BLURB

My best friend is happily coupled up with the girl of his dreams and all he asked me to do is help keep her safe. Her and her friend.

I can do that. I'm a bodyguard. Protection is what we do.

But how the hell do you protect someone like JJ? Loud, argumentative and more sass than sense. I learned a long time ago that protection and romance don't mix but JJ is a crack in my armor. An argumentative, beautiful crack in my armor.

And to protect her I might have to break the vow I made years ago.

Book 1 of The Force Duet.

FORCE

M. MALONE

NANA MALONE

CONTENTS

FORCE

Noah watched Rafe through the window. His future brother-in-law stood silent sentry over the rest of the clan. Even on the occasion of his beloved sister's wedding, he held himself separate. Not out of reach in case he was needed, but still, not part of the group. An outsider.

Maybe this is a mistake.

No. It wasn't a mistake. Rafe DeMarco was his brother. *Had* always been his brother, his teacher. Even if he was different now.

Noah rubbed the back of his neck. He knew it was true. Rafe had seen things, done things. He'd been out in the cold too long. Without friends, without family. Rafe had never come out and expressed anything, but knowing the kind of undercover work he'd done, Noah could imagine how he felt.

He didn't want his brother to be separate from them anymore. It was time to do the right thing. The only real question was how the others would take it. They worked for him, but in essence, Blake Security ran like a family. And likely, each of them would have something to say about his decision.

Also, seeing as Rafe had tried to kill them all, some of them might still be holding grudges.

Luckily, it was just that one time. Okay, it might have been a couple of times. Rafe was sorry though, right?

Maybe not as sorry as he should be.

Noah pushed into the waiting room. Jonas greeted him with a grin. "There he is. We were starting to wonder if you'd executed plan Condor."

Noah frowned. "What the fuck is plan Condor?

Dylan eyed him knowingly. "It's a plan where you take flight like a bird."

Noah rolled his eyes. "Do you have any idea how long I waited to have Lucia? I'm not going anywhere." He frowned. "Though, now I feel like I should have one of you make sure *she* doesn't run."

Oskar rolled his eyes. "Well if JJ is planning the escape, they're already gone."

Noah frowned. Lucia's best friend JJ was a known troublemaker and had a mouth like a sailor, but even *she* couldn't convince Lucia to turn runaway bride. Could she?

No dumbass. They're just rattling your cage.

Rafe frowned. "If she doesn't want to get married, we're certainly not going to force her."

"Have you met your sister? When was the last time she did anything that she didn't precisely want to do?"

Rafe chuckled. "Yeah, you have a point about that."

"Can I borrow you for a minute, Rafe?" Noah kept his voice low, but the atmosphere in the room changed in a heartbeat.

Rafe gave him a terse nod before saying, "Yeah of course."

Once Noah had him out of the vestibule and into the courtyard of the church, Rafe was all business. "What's up man?"

"You know what I want to ask you, right?"

Rafe nodded. "I could see you've been working up to it. But I'll tell you the truth, it's a little late for strippers. My sister would kill me."

Noah chuckled. "As if you would let me get strippers."

"Yeah, of course. I mean I would just hire the same crew of jocks that she hired for you last time. That shit would be funny."

"Man, she told you about that?"

Rafe chuckled. "Yep. Now I know what to get you for every birthday for the rest of your life."

"And here I thought we were brothers."

Rafe grinned, and for a second he looked much more like the man who'd trained Noah. The man who'd taught him everything he knew. "That is precisely why I'm getting you strippers every birthday. What are big brothers for?"

Noah laughed. "You know, that's a good point."

"So what's up Noah? It's not like you to have cold feet."

Noah slanted him a look. "You do know me." He rubbed his jaw, unsure what to do with the sudden influx of nerves. "Look, I know you've got your own deal with the FBI and your undercover assignments with Interpol. But I think maybe you've been doing that too long. Maybe it's time to come back into the fold. Family, friends, and all that."

Rafe had always been hard to read. He was an inscrutable bastard. But Noah pressed on. "Look, it's probably clear to you I need help. I've got more work than I have men for, and I'm spread thin. We've taken a lot of hits this past year. Ryan and Dylan are great, but I need someone who can take them to the next level. Matthias is good, but he's too on edge to be a teacher. I could use someone who actually knows how to train agents. But you know, *not* for wet work."

Rafe shook his head. "You try to kill a guy one time, and he never lets that shit go."

Noah chuckled. "Well, it was more than one time. Let's face it, you very nearly killed me."

"Well, you actually *did* kill me." At Noah's wince, Rafe chuckled. "Too soon?"

Noah nodded. "Yeah man, too soon. I'm not used to having you back yet." Noah sighed. This felt good. Like those years between them vanished. Up until now, he hadn't known what to say. "Seriously though. We always think about it. I —" he cleared his throat. "Not just for Lucia, but for me. I... missed you."

Noah met Rafe's gaze. He would have sworn he saw a glimmer of hope. Maybe longing.

Rafe rocked back on his heels. "You know, I think I've had enough of the FBI. Obviously, I would never go back to ORUS. I never wanted to be in anyway. But that blood on my hands, Noah... it's not a small thing."

Noah nodded. "I know. But if I can do it, you can. It's pretty easy actually. The jobs you go on, you're almost guaranteed to come home from."

Rafe shrugged. "Sounds boring. Can't you throw in a starlet or something?"

Noah chuckled. "I'll see what I can do, man. You might have to wrestle Dylan for starlet duty though."

"To hear Dylan talk about it, it's like he'd rather face a firing squad."

"I don't know what he has against pop princesses. I swear that was one of my favorite assignments."

Rafe nodded. "I've lost too much time with Lucia and Nonna. Other people, too."

Noah rolled his eyes. "Just say it man, you missed me. Go on, you know you want to."

"Yeah, whatever. You can use some extra training. Next time go for the kill shot."

Noah shook his head. "Fuck man, still too soon."

"Speaking of too soon, how do think the band of misfits in there is gonna take it?"

Noah sighed. "Oh, they'll follow along. But could you maybe try to refrain from dislocating any shoulders or killing anyone? You know, for a while."

"There you go, ruining all my fun."

It felt good bantering with Rafe. Noah's heart might burst he was so happy. But he sobered quickly. "About Matthias though."

Rafe's good-natured attitude melted off his body. "Is he tight? Because he looks like he's riding that edge."

Noah nodded. "He had it bad before he even got to ORUS, and I don't know, I might not have gotten him out soon enough. That killer instinct is right below the surface, you know?"

"The way he fights, he's good. A complete natural."

Noah nodded. "Unless absolutely necessary, I've benched him from any violent shit. Only time I let him out in the field is for his unique expertise or if I really think some people could get killed. He's a good kid, and he's never had a fair shot."

Rafe nodded. "I'll give him a wide berth for a bit. Give him a chance to settle down and get used to me." He paused for a moment and slid him a glance. "We good?"

Noah nodded. "Yeah. We're good. You helped me when I was going off the rails, and I've never said thank you for that."

Rafe nodded and drew in a deep breath. "And I never said I was sorry."

Noah frowned. "For what?"

"You are my brother. And you're about to be my brother-in-law in just a little under an hour —"

Noah shook his head. "Man, it's not necessary."

"Yes, it is. I feel like I'm in Assassins Anonymous or some shit. But I do need to make amends. I'm sorry for the guilt you had to carry around. If there had been any other way to protect the two of you, I would have taken it."

Shit, were his eyes stinging? "I understand. I just wish —"

Rafe's brows drew up. "Yeah?"

"I just wish we didn't have so much time to make up for."

Rafe nodded and swiped a knuckle under his eye. "Yeah. Me too. So, what do you say we get back to the assholes so you can break the news to them real easy, like a couple of anal virgins."

Noah shook his head. "Way inappropriate man. Seems like you'll fit right in."

———

"Okay guys, I wanted to talk to you about something before the wedding. Things have been busier than ever this past year. It's time to expand."

Jonas narrowed his gaze. "Yeah? How many are we taking on? We're spread thin already, and training can be kind of a bitch."

Noah nodded. "I hear you. That's why we're only taking on one new guy. And I guarantee you, training won't be necessary."

Matthias's gaze ping-ponged between Noah and Rafe. "Nah, mate. Tell me you're not fucking thinking what I *think* you're thinking about."

Dylan slid his gaze back and forth between Noah and Matthias. "Huh? What am I missing?"

Oskar crossed his arms and hung his head, shaking it backward and forward. "You don't see it? Noah is asking this one to join the team." He jerked his thumb in Rafe's direction.

Rafe, to his credit, didn't budge. Didn't move, didn't smile, frown or anything.

Matthias however was far less cool. "Over my fucking dead body, mate."

Rafe muttered under his breath. "That can be arranged."

Of course that got Matthias's hackles up. He took a step toward Rafe, and Oskar had to physically stop him.

Dylan shook his head. "No. Not doing it. Not working with this asshole. Dude, have you forgotten he tried to kill us? More than once?"

Rafe smirked. "Trust me, if I'd actually wanted you dead, you would be dead."

Noah shook his head. "Rafe, not fucking helping."

Ryan chuckled. "I can't believe this. You're actually thinking about asking this turd to join the team. I know he's Lucia's brother and all but, I don't like it."

As the members of his team grumbled, Noah could see the loneliness, the confusion, and what he thought might be a faint glimmer of hope. "Okay, you idiots, you've had the opportunity to express your displeasure. Not that I give two shits. Do you all trust me?"

Matthias was the first to meet his gaze. The kid may not be happy about what Noah was saying right now, but after everything that had happened between them, Noah knew he had Matthias's loyalty, no matter what. When he spoke, his voice was barely above a growl. "Through fire," he said quietly.

Noah nodded. Honestly, he hadn't even had to ask. Although, it might be one hell of a task trying to keep the two of them from killing each other. Matthias was somewhat untested, but in some ways he was just as deadly as Rafe. Dylan just threw up his hands. "Are you fucking serious right now?"

Next to Dylan, Ryan clenched his jaw. "Yeah boss, you know I do, especially after what you've done for me, but —"

Noah shook his head. "No buts. You either trust me, or you don't."

Ryan swallowed but then nodded, unable to even look at him.

Considering where Noah had found Ryan, the kid was a sure bet, too.

Dylan was a wildcard. As was Oskar. Not that Noah didn't think Oskar would do the right thing, but rather because the German was somewhat of a wildcard all the time. He always had his own motivations for doing things. Yet he always wanted to do the *right* thing. And if he thought you were doing that, he'd follow without question. And then there was Jonas. His best friend. The friend who'd been left to pick up the pieces of his shattered soul. The friend who he lied to for years, but who he'd eventually been forced to come clean with about who he was. Jonas was also the friend who'd helped him heal.

And you saved him too. There'd been a moment in time when Jonas had been sitting in front of the gates of hell. And then Noah's skills had come in handy. But honestly, if Noah was being honest with himself, his friend had saved him more than he helped his friend.

Jonas slid his gaze to Noah and nodded. "I don't like it. I'm not a fan." He glanced briefly over to Rafe. "But he's Lucia's brother, which means he'll do anything to keep his sister safe. And she is our family, so I'm assuming that extends to us. And then, well, you're vouching for him. So I may not understand it, but I'll back your play. Although," he turned to face Rafe and stared him down, "you try any of that shit again, and I will kill you in your sleep."

Rafe smirked. "Again, you're welcome to try."

Noah could only chuckle. That was Rafe for you. Because at the end of the day, everyone in the room knew that if Rafe wanted to, he could put them all down.

Dylan dropped his hands. "Seriously? Whatever man. If

you say he's on the team, he's on the team. I'll work with him. But that's only because I trust you."

Noah nodded. Oskar only chuckled. "Why the fuck not? Hell, since these guys are pussies anyway, I'll volunteer to train him."

"Like I need your fucking training," Rafe growled.

"See in the real world, you can't go around killing people and shit. I know you former assassins have a problem with that. But it's not really what we do here. So I'm happy to teach you the finer points of security. You know... *not* killing the clients and shit."

Rafe considered this. "Yeah, you might have a point. I am better at killing things."

Oskar just shook his head. "You see, my training skills are at work already."

Noah turned his gaze to his friend, the man he'd call brother in under an hour. "Welcome back to the fold."

———

10 Months Later...

Jessica Jones closed her eyes, exhausted. Day after draining day of pulling double duty while her bestie and partner in crime was on maternity leave was starting to take its toll. Like hell was she going to start complaining, though. If anyone deserved happiness, it was Lucia. Her best friend had been to hell and back and deserved the time off.

JJ could deal. After all Lucia would do it for her. Besides, JJ wasn't letting a prima donna fashion designer run her into the ground and call uncle. She'd rather burn her Jimmy Choos first. She could handle anything their boss Adriana could dish out.

It felt like she'd only shut her eyes for mere seconds before she frowned in her sleep.

Something was wrong. *Very* wrong.

When she peeled her eyes open again, she was in hell.

"Oh my god," she screamed.

But that scream was her first mistake. It meant emptying out her lungs, which meant she needed to breathe... and that meant lungs full of smoke.

It was so hot her hair plastered against her head and her

sheets clung to her naked breasts from sweat. Yeah, she slept topless, so what? It had been so hot lately.

Frantic, she looked around the room trying to find the source of heat. It was so dark she couldn't see anything. But she could feel the smoke all around her, cloying and thick, wrapping around her and constricting her lungs.

"Don't panic." The sound of her own voice out loud scared her out of her frozen state. *Fear immobilizes. Anger motivates.* That's right, get pissed off!

If there was anything JJ was good at, it was being hot tempered. What the fuck was smoke doing in her room anyway? She'd just had a goddamned blowout. She needed to charge that color and cut to whatever or whoever was the source of this fire.

Move your ass girly.

She had to move because she was *not* dying in this room. She did not survive her past to die like this. Fuck that noise. Besides, if she died like this, Lucia would resurrect her ass and kill her all over again. After Lucia had survived being stalked and almost killed, JJ had a new appreciation for the meaning of life.

She swung her legs over the side of the bed, letting out a sigh of relief when her toes met the carpet. Now that her eyes had adjusted to the dark somewhat, she could see the faint hint of an orange glow from down the hall. Which meant the fire hadn't reached her room... yet.

But the bedroom door stood open to the hall, which was probably why she could already smell the smoke.

It was weird that the door was open. She always closed the door before going to sleep. It was one of the things Lucia's husband had drilled into her. Noah owned a security company, and his overprotectiveness toward Lucia had spilled over onto JJ. Now she always had one of the annoying, albeit sexy, guys who worked for him trailing her to and from work, and her apartment had been subjected to a thorough security 'review' by Noah's resident IT wizard. Matthias had deemed her place 'merely acceptable.'

JJ was pretty sure they'd have asked her to move if they hadn't known from experience that she didn't take suggestions well. The last thing she needed was some man trying to tell her what to do. Maybe Lucia was okay with that, but she wasn't interested. JJ knew from experience that she didn't want any man having control over her life. Never again. That alpha-asshole shit didn't work for her, so they could shove their over protectiveness where the sun didn't shine.

With a quick glance at the open door, she realized it was actually lucky she'd left it open, otherwise she might not have woken up until the flames were closer. What the hell had woken her? *You can think through that shit after you're safe.* Yeah, good point. She grabbed up her comforter and wrapped herself in the thick fabric, bringing it up over her head as she stepped into a pair of slippers.

How far to the door? The window might be an option if the fire escape hadn't been welded over some years ago. She looked up and then squinted in the darkness. And then she saw the shadow in the hall. The man-sized shadow.

Fuck me. She opened her mouth to scream then reached into her bedside drawer for the nearest weapon she could find. She'd been aiming for the retractable baton she kept in the top drawer. But instead she'd come up with a gag gift from a bachelorette party a couple of years ago. A giant purple vibrator.

What are you gonna do with that? Fuck him to death? Well that was a thought.

"Who the hell are you? And what the fuck are you doing in my apartment?"

He stepped forward slightly, his body still half-hidden outside the door, and JJ raised her makeshift weapon.

"I'm here for you, Jessica. I'm always here for you."

JJ clutched the blanket closer, and her fingers curled around the vibrator as his voice washed over her. The low tone of his words sliced through her veins. That voice. It had been so long since she'd heard that voice. She'd hoped to never hear it again, except in her nightmares.

"How did you find me?"

His chuckle was almost as terrifying as the words that followed. "I never lost you."

JJ screamed and backed up so fast that she stumbled and fell on the bed. The comforter tangled around her and she fought against it, certain the next touch she'd feel would be the last.

Strong hands wrapped around her flailing arms.

"Damn it, you crazy woman, I'm trying to help you!"

It took a few seconds before she recognized the voice, her terror distorting it into the one she feared most. When she finally spoke, her voice was tiny.

"Jonas? Is that you?"

The comforter was pulled back away from her eyes, and Jonas's handsome face appeared. Jonas Castillo worked for Noah's security company and was a regular fixture in her life. He was routinely assigned to protect Lucia, and by default JJ, during the workweek. She took great pleasure in giving him hell, and he was usually cursing her name or bickering with her.

"Yes, of course it's me."

Before she could question what he was doing there, she felt herself being lifted. She clutched his shoulders automatically, disoriented after her fall. Now she wasn't sure if that had actually happened. Had she been dreaming? It was so hard to tell.

"Jonas, did you see anyone else in the apartment?"

"Like who? Don't you live alone?"

Was that jealousy in his voice? Even under these circumstances, JJ couldn't resist the urge to screw with him a little.

"Actually I don't. We can't leave without my favorite guy."

"Who? And if you have a boyfriend, where is he? Some help he is during an emergency."

"Well, Fluffy has never been much help during emergencies, but he blows the best wet kisses."

Jonas didn't pause. "I'll come back for your dog, I promise. But I have to get you to safety."

It must have been the smoke affecting her brain, because at first JJ didn't realize what he'd said. It wasn't until they were at the front door that she understood he meant to leave.

"No! I have to get Fluffy!" JJ swatted at his massive chest. She must have surprised him because his arms loosened around her legs, giving her the room she needed to jump down.

"Damn it, JJ! This is serious. We don't have time to stop."

"It'll just take a second." JJ raced back to the guest bedroom and grabbed Fluffy, covering him with the comforter as she ran.

Jonas picked her up as soon as she hit the hallway and ran for the front door. They passed a crew of firefighters in the corridor outside her apartment. The smoke was thicker out here, so JJ buried her face in Jonas's shoulder, making sure to keep Fluffy covered too.

When they got outside, Jonas set them down carefully on the grass, safely away from the building. An EMT approached, and Jonas pointed at JJ. She was going to protest, but dissolved into a coughing fit as soon as she opened her mouth. The young man frowned and knelt on the grass next to her. Then his eyes widened when her comforter slipped and she almost flashed an entire boob at him.

"Hey, eyes up, kid." Jonas glared at him before yanking his shirt off. He put it over JJ's head, and she maneuvered carefully to get her arms in without dropping the comforter completely. If she hadn't felt so crappy, she'd have told him exactly where he could shove it. She didn't need anyone speaking for her.

Just to annoy him, she gave the EMT a bright smile that

had the young man blushing furiously. Jonas scowled at both of them.

After a flurry of activity, blood pressure cuffs, and oxygen, they finally left her alone. That's when Jonas got a good look at her again. Her *and* Fluffy.

"A fish? You risked your life to save a fucking fish?"

JJ scooped up Fluffy's bowl protectively. "Fluffy is not just a fish. He's a Japanese fighting fish. A total badass."

Jonas looked like he wanted to strangle her. Normally that was exactly the effect she was going for, but strangely, it wasn't as satisfying as usual.

"Thank you, Jonas. For coming in after me."

He looked as shocked as she felt by her sudden gratitude.

"Of course. It's nothing. The fire department would have gotten to you soon. I just happened to get there first when Matthias said your alarms were triggered."

The talk of alarms brought back memories of the man she'd seen in the smoke. It had happened so fast, and she couldn't be sure what was real and what had been a dream.

"Did you see anyone in there?" At his confused look, JJ clarified, "In my apartment?"

Jonas knelt and looked her in the eye. "Was there someone in there with you, Jessica?"

It was all such a blur, and she didn't like the way he was looking at her. Noah's entire crew was extremely overprotective, so if she said the wrong thing, she'd end up on house arrest with Jonas as her jailor. Plus, it was likely it had all been a dream. Jonas had been in her apartment. He would have seen if anyone else was there. The man in the smoke was nothing more than a shadow from a past she'd rather forget.

"No, I meant in the building. I just want to make sure all my neighbors got out okay."

Jonas looked like he wanted to say something else, but Noah arrived just then with Lucia right behind him.

JJ accepted a hug from her friend, and that was when it really hit her.

"I guess I'm homeless now."

Noah's voice carried from behind Lucia. "You'll stay with us, of course."

JJ's eyes met Jonas's, and she knew he was thinking about her earlier question.

"It's for the best," Jonas said.

She glanced over at Lucia. "Free rent and a house full of hot men. Count me in."

CHAPTER ONE

She was lying to him.

Jonas Castillo eyed his client, Mira Ashton, carefully. She'd been beaten and abused by her ex-husband for years. She was still cagey around men. But since he was one of the people who'd gotten her away from that asshole, she shouldn't be afraid of him. So why was this whole situation off?

He'd met her at the café just on the edge of the theater district as she'd asked him to. Normally, they would do a site visit at her home but given her history, he didn't think anything was unusual about her asking to meet him here. But now he wasn't sure.

Something wasn't right.

"Mira, you sure you're okay?"

Her gaze snapped to his. "I'm fine. It's just that it's really crowded in here."

"We don't have to stay here. If you would like, I can drive you back to your apartment." She lived about three or four blocks from here.

Her eyes went wide. "No. This is fine."

"Are you sure? Did your husband call? If you're scared or unsure, we can help with that. That's the purpose behind these check-ins. We do this for all our clients. It's no trouble at all for us to look into another matter for you if someone's bothering you."

She shook her head. "It's nothing like that. I just—I just hate that I needed you in the first place. That I got myself into the situation. That's not who I am; that's not me. I don't like how everything turned out, but I'm fine. I just have to learn how to deal."

He nodded. "It's going to take some time. Just know that he can't hurt you. We got him out of the house. And you got a restraining order against him. It's not in his best interest to come near you. If he breaks that restraining order, he goes back to jail. He doesn't want that. So you're safe."

She shifted her gaze away from his. "Yeah. Safe."

Jonas's brow furrowed again. "Can I get you another slice of pie? Something else to eat?"

"No. I think I'm just going to head home."

"Okay, let me give you a ride. I parked just across the street."

For a long moment her gaze lifted and met his, holding it. It was as if she wanted to tell him something. Wanted him to hear something. But what the hell was she trying to say?

"No, I think I'm just going to walk."

He wanted to argue with that. But she set her jaw, and he'd seen that look before. It was the I'm-not-fucking-around look. It was the look people got when they set their minds about something and had no intention of changing them. "All right. You have a good night now, okay?"

She scooted out of the booth and stood. "I will. Thank you for everything. You don't know—" She cut herself off and sighed deeply before continuing. "You, all of you at Blake Security, you don't know what you have done for me. Thank you."

Jonas waited exactly thirty seconds before he followed her. He had no idea who the hell Noah had to blow to get special curbside parking access around most of the city, but all of Blake Security's cars were equipped with special plates and they could park anywhere. Farther down the block, she hopped into a taxi.

It took her the few blocks to her apartment. Jonas figured she might not have wanted to deal with the summertime crowds in the theater district, as it was packed.

When she reached her apartment, she climbed out of the cab and stared up at the building for a moment. Jonas parked across the street and watched her intently. And then he saw what she was looking at. Someone passed in front of the front window. Someone was walking around.

Jonas's eyes narrowed. It wasn't so much that she had a guest that had him concerned. It was that he recognized the movement of that guest. The guy was mostly in shadow, but Jonas recognized the way he walked and rolled his shoulders. That was her ex-husband. What the fuck was he doing in her house?

Mira's building didn't have a doorman. Luckily, he had a key. He tried to wait patiently until she was up the elevator before following in the service elevator behind her. It was farther down the hall than her apartment, but he'd be able to observe her. *Stalker much?* Damn it, he just wanted to make sure she was okay.

You need to let this go. She's not Emma.

He shoved away the painful memory of the woman he'd tried to help all those years ago. The one he'd been unable to help. The one that had cost him his career. Probably better if he didn't think about her right now.

He shook it off. Mira wasn't Emma. For starters, he could help Mira. He watched from the shadows as she stuck the key in the lock, but the door opened on its own and she was dragged inside. Just as he was about to head down the hallway, the door to the stairway opened and someone stepped out, grabbed him, and yanked him into the stairwell.

He dislodged the grip in less than a second and had his hands up, ready to fight. It took him a moment longer to realize he knew the asshole who was trying to pick a fight. "Noah? What the fuck?"

"Jonas, I was in the area and Matthias notified me that

your GPS was headed to Mira's house. Did she meet you at the café?"

"Yeah, dumbass, she did." Jonas ran a hand through his hair. "But she was acting cagey and weird. So I wanted to make sure she was okay and got home safe. There's a guy in her apartment right now."

Noah sighed. "I know."

"What do you mean you know?" Jonas glared at him.

"Look, when Matthias came to check in on her last week, he noticed her ex in the doorway. She hugged him, kissed him. They're back together."

"Son of a bitch."

Jonas tried to yank open the stairwell door, but Noah stopped him. "You need to follow the Disney princess's advice and let it go. Mira made her choice."

No, this wasn't Noah talking. "We got her away from him. He has to have something on her, be scaring her or something."

Noah shook his head. "No. We've tailed her for over a week. She's back with him."

"We have to do something. After everything we did to get

her away from him, after everything we went through to keep her safe ... "

"I know. But this is her choice. You can't want something for her she doesn't want for herself. You have to let it go. We can't intervene unless she asks us to."

Jonas shoved him. He had to help her. Problem was, Noah was just as big as he was. Not to mention the guy was good. Assassin good. But that didn't stop Jonas from fighting with him. He had to get to her.

"Look man, you're one of my best friends. I'm happy to fight with you so you can let off some steam, but this is a fight you can't win. Not with me, or with her. She is making her choice. You can't make it for her."

Noah's last words finally sank in. He couldn't make her choices for her. So just like before, all he could do was stand by and watch as someone he cared about set herself on a path for disaster.

He sagged against the wall and Noah clapped him on the shoulder. "This is bullshit."

"I know. But how about we focus on the people we can actually help? We'll be here when she comes back. But for now, let her go."

Jonas glanced up at him. He knew what Noah was saying. But he had zero intention of letting this go. Sometimes people needed to be saved from themselves.

———

"All I'm saying is that he's a pain in the ass. I mean, can you believe that he told me I was being a prima donna? *Me*. A prima donna!" Jessica Jones spun around on her stool as she watched her best friend style a mannequin for an upcoming fashion show. "I'm the least prima donna person I know." A quick glance at the mannequin told her what she needed to style the makeup for the upcoming fashion show. "Actually, maybe go with the orange belt? I can do a really pretty gold shimmer with that."

Lucia Blake raised an eyebrow at her. "JJ, I have *no idea* why he would call you a prima donna," she said with a smirk.

JJ rolled her eyes. "Okay, I like things a certain way. There's nothing wrong with that."

Lucia giggled. "And I'm not saying that there is. I'm saying I think you and Jonas like to push each other's buttons. Why don't you just give in and say you like him already?"

"I do *not* like him. Matter of fact, I *hate* him." Never mind that half the time she wanted to pick a fight with him just because he got her blood pumping. And also, never mind the fact that her lady parts throbbed every time he gave her one of his annoying smirks.

"I mean just because he thinks he saved my life, it doesn't mean he can say whatever he wants to me. Bigger men than him have tried." Except that wasn't true. Jonas was big, and she actually liked the way he talked to her.

"Honey, he *did* actually save your life," Lucia pointed out oh so helpfully.

JJ shuddered when she remembered the fire that had razed her apartment to ash. It had nearly consumed her too. She'd been asleep in her bedroom when the fire had started.

The memory of feeling like she was choking made her stomach turn. She hadn't been able to wake up at first, almost like she'd taken a sleeping pill or something. Next thing she knew, Jonas was bursting through her bedroom door even as smoke licked at him from the living area.

Management had said it was an electrical fire. Her building had been renovated about fifteen years prior, but they said something went wrong with the wiring between the trio of apartments on the corner. Her place took the brunt of the damage, so now she was living at Blake Security headquarters. The view at the penthouse was better, but she missed her own space.

"Okay, fine, you have a point. He did save my life, but he's still a caveman. And a jackass. Saving my life does not preclude that."

Lucia snorted. "You may have a point."

The man was just so damned frustrating. She wanted to hit him, *and* she wanted to jump his bones. She knew that wasn't a healthy response. So she was just going to keep that to herself. Besides, her history with men involved picking exactly the wrong kind of guy. And Jonas was the wrong kind of guy. Besides, he hated her just as much as she hated him.

Which isn't very much at all.

She shoved that thought down. So what if she occasionally busted out her battery-operated boyfriend when she was thinking about him in her bed alone at night. So? Lots of women did that. It didn't mean she was a glutton for punishment or that she was ever going to do anything about it.

Yeah, you just keep telling yourself that.

"I mean just because he and his boys are part of some secret government hit squad doesn't mean he's so cool."

Lucia's eyes bugged, and JJ stared at her. Her best friend was no good at lying or keeping secrets usually. She would never blurt it out, but ask her a direct question and she was toast ... every time.

"Holy shit, are you kidding me right now?"

Lucia flushed. "Given everything you've seen in the last year, you know you need to keep that to yourself right?"

Lucia didn't have to tell her twice. "I'm not an idiot. Usually the people coming after us have very big guns. So fine. He is part of a secret government hit squad. I mean talk about #squadgoals."

A laugh burst out of her best friend. "You're ridiculous."

JJ grinned. "Take that Taylor Swift. My squad is hotter than your squad."

Their boss Adriana poked her head into the styling room. "There you are."

JJ and Lucia both glanced up to look at her. Adriana had that kind of former-model's body that any stylist would be thrilled to dress. Long lean lines, with high cheekbones and a beautifully sculpted face. She was fifty and looked like she was thirty-five. JJ had no idea how she did that. She figured she must use some seriously expensive European creams.

She grinned up at her. "What's up boss lady? Lucia is just finishing the styling, and I'll have the final makeup color palette for you, probably this afternoon."

Lucia nodded. "JJ suggested using the orange belt. I like that one. Or maybe this one that's a little more salmon. JJ, that'll work for you right?"

JJ nodded. "Yeah, that works too. I have a really pretty peach shimmer I can use that will still work."

Adriana agreed. "Use Lucia as a test model. She has that gorgeous olive skin and we can see how it all works together. But that's not why I'm here, actually."

"What do you need?" JJ asked.

"This year we're working with a new charity, Hope Springs. It's for domestic violence survivors. I'd love for you to be instrumental in this. I want you to sit down with the board and help map out the campaign. There are a lot of women who have just managed to leave their situations. A lot of them still bear scars and need some help to get back on their feet. But it's sort of impossible to even try to go back to work when you're covered in bruises and scars.

"We wanted to do a benefit makeup campaign; raise funds, raise awareness, and then train makeup artists on how to help these women put on a brave face. A *survivor's* face. And every woman knows that you always feel a little better with makeup. The best part about this is we're pairing with some lower-cost makeup lines, so we want to do some simple looks that will work to get these women back in the workforce. Some of the work that you did with that homeless teenagers' charity last year was amazing. Some quick, simple, and cheap solutions. I think you're just the person."

As Adriana spoke, JJ's gut curled in on itself. All she could hear were Adriana's words clanging around her head. *Abused women. Domestic violence.* She couldn't do this. There was no way. She cleared her throat before she spoke. "I mean, sure, that sounds like a great cause, but is there any reason *I* need to sit with the board and help them? They can just repurpose what I used for the homeless teenagers. It would be a lot of the same work."

Adriana raised a brow and Lucia slid her a glance. JJ

wished she could explain to her best friend, but she just couldn't. This was not something she could talk about. And it was certainly not anything she could be involved with. It hit too close to home.

Even though Adriana had her brow raised, she carried on. " You're the best makeup stylist I have. And doing pro bono charity work is really important to the organization. I'll tell them to expect a call from you this afternoon."

Adriana left without another word. And she could do that because, well, she owned the joint. All she had to do was put down an edict, and she should expect for her word to become bond. The problem was this was the last thing on earth JJ wanted to do. She didn't want to go back to that time in her life. A time when she'd had to cover her physical and emotional bruises. She didn't want to think about the girl she'd been.

You can do this. This is your job. This is your dream job. Make it happen. One way or another.

When Adriana left, Lucia studied the two belts, the orange and salmon ones, holding them up to the mannequin. She didn't look over at her, but her tone said it all. "You okay, JJ?"

JJ forced a smile into her voice. "Of course I am." *I have to be.*

"You don't have to do that with me. But it's not like you to turn down a job Adriana gives you, especially since this is the kind of thing that you love to do. And secondly, why would you say no to something like this? It's a really great cause." Lucia turned to face her. "What's up?"

"I told you. Nothing. And it *is* a great cause. You're right. And of course I am going to do it. It just seems like I'd be repeating work I've already done, ya know?" The lie sounded clunky to her ears. She had to get out of there before Lucia saw through the lie for the excuse it was. That was the problem when you worked with your child-hood best friend. She could see through anything.

JJ wished she could tell her. She really did. But there were some things better left in the past. And the things she'd been through were some of them. "See you later, okay?" she muttered as she escaped the styling room before Lucia could respond.

Now she'd just have to figure out how the hell she was going to get out of this project.

CHAPTER TWO

Jonas had considered taking Noah up on his offer of a fight. Seriously considered it. But there was something about hitting a guy who was truly, deeply happy that sucked all the fun out of it.

He'd started imagining what would happen when they got back to the office, and Noah's wife saw their black eyes and bruised knuckles. They'd have to explain what had happened and then Lucia would fuss over the both of them, caught between her outrage that they were fighting like schoolboys and her compassion for their abused client.

In the end, he'd decided the release of steam wouldn't even be worth it. He chuckled darkly. Damn, they'd all gotten soft as of late. Being around a woman who loved him, albeit one that loved him like a sister, made a man soft.

He decided to take a walk instead.

Noah had offered to keep him company, but that would have just led them back to the aforementioned fight scenario. So he'd taken off alone, making sure to get as far away from Mira's building as possible. He'd been so charged with righteous fury that by the time he looked up again, he'd walked all the way back to the East Village. With a calmer head, he doubled back to get his car. By the time he made it back to the office, it was almost midnight.

He parked in his marked space in the underground garage at Blake Security and sat there in the dark for a minute before getting out, trying to get his head back on straight before he went upstairs and had to see anyone. It shouldn't have hit him so hard, seeing Mira with that asshole. He'd been a cop for a long time and had worked in security ever since his time with the force. It shouldn't surprise him at all that people often made bad decisions under pressure. But in this case, it had been like a boot to the face.

Because you thought you'd saved this one.

He shook off the dark thought as he got out of his car. It

was quiet and still on the parking level but he scanned the perimeter of the garage anyway. Always vigilant. Never let your guard down. He stayed on high alert as he crossed to the elevator bank and leaned forward so the retinal scanner could verify his identity. As he rode the elevator up to the top floor, he could only hope that no one was still awake. He just needed to grab his laptop.

Noah had decided that having a certain number of their team living on site was for the best, but Jonas was putting off the communal living deal for a while—at least formally. He liked his space, but the truth was he crashed at the penthouse more often than not.

Surprisingly it wasn't all bad. There was always someone around to shoot the breeze with and his workload seemed lighter since he wasn't spending valuable time in the morning and afternoon commuting. He probably should just give in and move in already.

But it was also exhausting having trained security agents watching your every move and analyzing everything you said. He couldn't just lounge in his pajamas when he felt like shit without having to answer a bunch of questions. They were a nosy bunch, his crew.

He loved them anyway.

The elevator doors slid open and Jonas stepped into the entryway. It was dark and quiet, the only sound coming from the direction of Matthias's room. That kid never slept no matter what time of day it was, but he also didn't ask questions. So he was off the hook.

Then he stepped into the living room and was confronted with a tight, toned ass in skintight leggings.

All the parts of him that had been asleep fired to life. Jonas sucked in a deep breath as JJ shifted her position at the window, the globes of her ass bouncing slightly with the movement. His dick tried to follow her. It should have been a welcome diversion. Hell, at least he wasn't depressed and feeling the sting of failure anymore. But this was JJ. The woman lived to torment him. So as spectacular as that ass was, it was the last thing he wanted to see in the middle of the night coming off a tough case.

"Why are you still awake?"

It came out harsher than he'd intended, but there was no need to apologize. JJ didn't offend easily, probably because she thrived on insults and could throw out verbal daggers with the best of them. As he'd expected, she merely turned her head slightly to acknowledge his presence before turning back to the night sky, dismissing him.

"Why can't *you* mind your own business?" she asked in a deceptively sweet voice.

Never mind that just a few moments ago, Jonas had wanted nothing more than to climb into bed without having to engage anyone. Now he stepped farther into the room, instinctively drawn to her. There was just something about Jessica Jones that he could not resist. It was sick in a way, but he got off on fighting with her. That smart mouth and those killer curves were the perfect combination to make his dick hard while simultaneously pissing him off.

It was a heady combination.

"What would be the fun in that?" Jonas asked, speaking truthfully.

She turned from whatever it was that was holding her attention outside and eyed him with a sneer. "I would ask if you had a hot date but that's doubtful. Jackasses really aren't in this season."

Now that hurt. "Women love me."

She sniffed and slid him a sidelong glance. "Frankly, I don't see the appeal. But then again there are people who like candy corn and Peeps. There's really no accounting for taste … or lack thereof."

"Hey! Candy corn is awesome." Jonas might have to rethink his taste in women if she was dogging on candy corn. How could you not enjoy something that was pure high-octane sugar? "You're probably just too bitter to enjoy it."

Her eyes flashed and for a moment there was something behind the look that made him regret his choice of words. "Too bad for you, you'll never have a taste." Her words carried a hint of hurt with them and he wanted to bite off his tongue.

They snarked at each other and played fast and loose with their words, but he would never actually want to hurt her. It bothered him that he even could. In his mind, JJ was as invincible as her comic book character namesake, and finding a chink in her armor was both disturbing and endearing.

"I'm sorry. I didn't mean anything by that."

"Whatever. You're probably right. I'll leave the sweetness to you. I just happen to like my men a little bit … stronger with a hint of a bite. Same way I like my whiskey."

When he looked up she was watching him closely.

"What?" he asked.

She shrugged. "Nothing. You just look ... never mind. I was enjoying some peace and quiet, but I think that ship has sailed. Good night."

He watched with a sinking feeling in his chest as she walked over to the couch and collected a blanket and a paperback book from the cushions. She did that frequently, curled up in a corner with a book and got lost in another world. It was one more thing about her that didn't compute with the smart mouth and the fuck-off attitude. Jonas would never have pegged her for a book-worm—more like a party girl every night of the week.

"Night," he called out.

She didn't respond or look back. Which bothered him more than he could say.

———

J could feel his eyes on her ass.

She could actually feel it, like a physical touch. It was an ingrained response to be annoyed by

Jonas, like swatting a fly or clearing your throat. But lately she'd had a harder time denying that having his eyes on her wasn't exactly ... horrible.

Oh, fine. It was arousing as hell to know that he couldn't stop looking at her ass. But that didn't mean she wanted him to know that.

She clutched her book tighter against her chest. It was such bullshit that he'd come in and ruined her night. It had been a perfectly fine day at work, crazy boss demands aside, but she'd been restless and dissatisfied all week. She'd been looking forward to a quiet night on the couch with a book and the stars. Then he'd come along and ruined it. What the hell was he doing coming in so late looking for a fight anyway?

Before she could question the wisdom of it, JJ spun on her heel and marched back down the hallway to the living room. She skidded to a stop as Jonas came into view. No longer in the middle of the room, he stood at the window with his forehead pressed to the glass. There was a wealth of pain in his expression, like he'd jump straight out that window and to the pavement below if it were possible.

JJ shifted uncomfortably, sure he wouldn't want her to see him so unguarded. Despite how much they bickered and how crazy he made her, the sight of him so unmoored brought her no joy. Yes, Jonas was an asshole. But strangely enough, she thought of him as *her* asshole. And no one messed with her friends.

"Do you ever have any regrets?" she asked.

He didn't move in any way, but there was a sudden tension in his shoulders that made her think he hadn't known she was there. That, in and of itself, was telling. Jonas had senses like a cat. She'd never been able to sneak up on him before. And she'd tried.

"Besides meeting you?"

JJ shook her head. Maybe it had been foolish to try to relate to him on a serious note. She and Jonas just didn't have that kind of relationship and there was no changing the rules now.

"I just thought ... Never mind. I'm going to bed. You can be a grumpy ass by yourself."

She turned to go, but before she could make it two steps, strong arms encircled her from behind. JJ sucked in a breath, caught off guard by how damn good it felt to be held like this. She turned her head slightly, freezing as her forehead brushed against his chin. He was tall and built, something she'd tried like hell not to notice before. But it was damn near impossible not to feel the rock-hard muscles behind her and around her. Or not to get lost in the warm masculine scent that drew her like a bumblebee to honey.

God, he even smells like testosterone. But in a good, nuzzle-into-his-neck-while-he-fucks-you-senseless-against-a-wall kinda way.

Her stomach clenched and there was an answering pull between her thighs. Damn it. She was not getting off on this.

"Let me go." She'd meant for it to come out bitchy as usual but there was a soft, plaintive note to her voice that made *let me go* sound suspiciously like *never let me go.*

"Sorry. I shouldn't have snapped at you like that. It's been a shitty day."

He walked back to the window and JJ immediately missed the warmth against her skin. She followed at a distance, still clutching her book and her blanket.

"You didn't lose a client, did you?" Belatedly she realized it was a terrible thing to ask. If he had, would he really want to talk about it?

But to her surprise, Jonas nodded. "Yeah. Not in the way you meant, but ... yeah. I lost one that I tried damn hard to save."

"I'm so sorry," JJ whispered, feeling for all the world like a complete waste of space. She'd been here snarking at him, and the whole time he was dealing with something serious.

Yes, her life was a shitstorm at the moment, but that didn't mean she was the only one with problems. When she looked up, Jonas was watching her with shrewd eyes.

"What's wrong with you?"

JJ shrugged. "Nothing is wrong with me."

As he continued to watch her with eyes that saw way too much, JJ suddenly wished she could tell him everything.

Why not tell Jonas? He works in security, after all. Maybe he can help.

But the same silly part of her had once believed that a restraining order would actually protect you, as well. And she knew from experience that was absolute bullshit. So as much as she wished she could tell him everything, she couldn't. Not that it wasn't tempting. Jonas was an asshole, but he was also really good at his job. She'd seen him with clients before, on the rare occasions they had to bring someone to the office. The women in particular loved him. He had a quiet sort of protectiveness that made you feel safe, yet heard. JJ had no doubt that he'd listen to her spill the whole story without judgment and then immediately come up with a plan for how to handle everything.

Maybe he'd even hold her again. It might be worth spilling her guts to feel those muscles wrapped around her again.

But it wouldn't be worth the humiliation. She'd worked so hard and come so far. Nothing from her past would ruin this for her. As hard as it was, JJ pasted on a smile and shook her head.

"There's nothing wrong with me. But it looks like there's something wrong with you." She pointed downward.

His eyes followed her finger, and he cursed under his breath. She felt like a bitch for pointing it out. After all, she'd had a physical reaction to him too, but her blanket was covering up her goose bumps and hard nipples.

"Anyway, I'm going to bed. Alone. But enjoy your hand tonight."

JJ turned and left him there alone with his hard-on. She tried to ignore the part of her that wanted to rush back there and give him a hand with it. Her past was coming back to haunt her, and she wouldn't take anyone else down with her.

Until she figured this whole thing out, it would be best if she kept her distance from everyone.

CHAPTER THREE

He really shouldn't like kicking ass so much. After all, he'd been a cop once before. But there was something really satisfying about beating the shit out of some stalking asshole. Yeah, maybe it was vigilantism, but the cops would be called in the end. After he was long gone.

Who have you become?

Jonas shoved the question away. He didn't want to think about that right now. And yeah, okay, he might be taking some of his irritation and aggression out on this guy. His mind still ran through the reel of having to watch Mira walk into her apartment, back to her ex. Back to the man who had beaten her so bloody she'd had to practically crawl into Blake Security for help.

And he was just supposed to let that shit go?

Never mind that though. The asshole of the evening was none other than Clint Evans. He'd been stalking a girl named Clara Cole for the last two years. Clara's family had come to Blake Security six months ago to try to resolve the situation. The police didn't have much to go on.

Clara had been smart, kept a diary of all the times she thought she was being watched. The problem was that Clint was also smart. Or the luckiest fucking asshole on earth. He'd managed to stay off the police radar. And there was no probable cause. So the cops couldn't just bust in and go looking through his stuff. And all the while, he kept terrorizing that poor girl. Well, now it was time for him to be terrorized.

Jonas advanced on him and the guy tried to crawl backwards. "I told you guys I'd leave her alone."

Jonas cracked his neck. "See, that's the thing. You said you were going to leave her alone last time my boys came to talk to you. But instead of leaving her alone, we found you at her swim meet. You realize the girl is sixteen, right?"

The turd in front of him swallowed hard, his hands

splashing into puddles as he scrambled to get away. "Look, she never told me she was sixteen."

"Did she *have* to tell you? After all, you were hanging around a high school when you first laid eyes on her."

"Don't make me sound like some kind of freak. I wasn't there for her. I was picking up my sister. Then I saw her. For all I knew she was eighteen. A senior, like my sister. So what? I've seen her around a few times. It's not a big deal."

Jonas just tsked. "No. No. No. You don't get to pretend like you had no idea. She was fourteen when you started stalking her. I've seen the pictures. She *looked* fourteen. *Real* young. So you don't get to pretend you had no idea how old she was. I mean, you even followed her on family vacations. Do you know what kind of sicko that makes you?" Jonas leaned close as he grabbed the guy by the shirt. "It makes you the kind of sick asshole that the guys in prison are gonna love."

The idiot's eyes widened. "I swear. I never touched her. It was just a coincidence that I went to Key West when her family did."

That's right Buddy. Keep painting me a picture. One of the key reasons the police hadn't been able to do much was because they couldn't prove that he was there. That Clint was everywhere Clara said he was. Because it was always just a feeling. Clara would think she saw him out of the corner of her eye, or swear that he was somewhere. But the bastard was good at hiding. Right now, as he rambled on and on about how being where she was had been just a coincidence, he was giving the police every-thing they needed.

"I love how you say you never touched her, but you sure terrorized her, all right. And when the cops search your place tonight, they're going to find all kinds of pictures of her. Pictures Photoshopped into suggestive positions. You're a sick bastard."

And because he couldn't help it, Jonas closed his hand into a fist and popped the fucker in the nose.

Goddamn, that felt good. *This isn't about Mira.* Again he shoved away any thoughts of the woman who didn't want his help. Instead, he focused on the guy in front of him who was now trying to run. Damn it, why did they always try to run?

The guy crawled a few feet and then pushed himself up onto his hands and knees, and finally to his feet. Jonas let him think he was going to get away, because really, what was the fun if he didn't get to chase him down?

Why couldn't they ever run when he was wearing tennis shoes? No, instead he was wearing his brand new Italian loafers. And the jackass wanted to splash around in fucking puddles.

You didn't have to wear your loafers tonight. Yes, that was a good point. But he liked to look sharp. Not to mention they'd had a client meeting earlier.

His mother had taught him that clothes help you make the best first impression. They didn't make the man, but they sure helped. It was a lesson he'd always carried with him close to his heart.

He didn't know he'd end up chasing after this asshole tonight, or he would have dressed for the occasion. He had a pair of four-hundred-dollar Nikes that would've gone great with a pair of black jeans and a black hoodie. So what? He liked shoes. *Don't judge me.*

"Dude, you're killing me with this running thing, and the splashing around in the puddles. Do you have any idea how much these shoes cost?"

He snatched the guy by the back of his shirt and dragged him around, slamming him into the brick wall of the alley. "Now come on. You must've seen where this was going. First, we have to track you down, and I'll give you credit: you're a slippery motherfucker. Next, we play nice and legal and get a restraining order. But like the *fucking idiot* you are, you still don't listen. One of my boys shows up a few weeks ago and warns you to never go near her again. And I know Oskar; he hates guys like you. You probably got his temper all up, and he hates that. It's not easy to get that guy to show emotion. Then we sent Matthias after you. You're lucky all he did was go after your bank accounts. That motherfucker could have killed you and not even blinked. Word is, Matthias left a lovely paper trail, so when the police come looking for you tonight, they're going to find all the evidence they need to prove you've been stalking Clara."

"You ... you ... you can't do that. You don't have any proof. I was careful. I follow her, but I don't touch her. It's not illegal to fantasize about hurting someone as long as you never do it."

Thanks asshole, that's just what we needed.

"No. We didn't. Not until just now." Jonas tapped the breast pocket that held the recorder. "I do appreciate you fessing up to stalking her. It helps. Especially when the cops are gonna find this in your back pocket."

The guy looked around. "I don't see the cops."

"Oh, another few minutes alone with me and you'll be wishing they were here already."

"Look, we can work out a deal. I'll leave town. I'll never come back again." The guy clutched Jonas's shirt, and Jonas dipped his head down to glare at the guy's grasp on his Brioni.

"I suggest you get your hands off my shirt. That's Brioni. You know that's a three-hundred-dollar shirt right?"

Asshole's brows furrowed. "What?"

"Yeah, you break it, you buy it, so I suggest you loosen your grip."

But the idiot didn't feel like listening. And he clutched tighter. "Look, I'll make you a deal. Whatever you want. It's yours. I cannot go to jail. I'm scared. I'm not gonna make it. I was in juvie once. Do you know the kind of crazy people they have in there?"

"You mean crazy like you? I can't wait until some big dude named Bubba starts stalking you around the yard. Watching your every move, plotting to hurt you. And maybe I'll give him a little nudge and tell him you like little girls."

The guy clutched tighter and tugged. Jonas heard the tear, and then muttered a curse under his breath. "Motherfucker. Are you fucking serious right now?"

He popped the guy in the nose again and his head clanked back against the wall, making him groan. "That was for the fucking shirt." Then Jonas hit him again. "And that's for not listening the first time." He released another fist. "And that's for trying to hurt a little girl." Jonas couldn't stop.

You're getting out of control again. Dial it back. Dial it back now!

But he was too far gone. His mind went completely quiet as he let pure instinct take over. Guys like this didn't deserve to walk the earth.

But then there was a voice in his earpiece. "While this is fun and all, listening to you beat this guy's ass," Matthias said, "I've got JJ on the move. You're the closest. It looks like she's leaving work, but she's not getting in a cab like she's supposed to. Can you swing by?"

Lucky for the idiot in his hands, Matthias had used the

magic word. *JJ*. She needed him a lot more than he needed to keep kicking ass.

"Yeah, I'm on it."

After Matthias disconnected, Jonas glanced down. "Damn it. I love this shirt," he muttered as he dragged Clint's limp body over to a light pole. He grabbed the recording device from his pocket and stuck it in Clint's back pocket after he wiped it down. And then he took a couple of zip ties and tied the douchebag to the pole.

The police would find enough information on Clint's stalking to put him away for a long time. And, in case that wasn't enough, they'd get a search warrant for his house, and find all the pictures of Clara Cole. That should do it. Back in the day, he hadn't liked the idea of being a vigilante. *But you're a long way from back in the day, aren't you?*

He wasn't going to go back there. He had a new life now. One that Noah had given him. And with that new life came the mouthy blonde he needed to go rescue from herself.

As he walked back to the car, not only did he have to wrangle the demons of his past, he had to wrangle the sexy blonde demon that ran through his skull. *JJ*. Just the idea of seeing her right now made the blood in his veins run hot.

And like the traitor it was, his goddamn dick twitched in his pants. He needed to get that shit under control. He didn't even like her. She was all mouth and a huge pain in the ass.

But there were times he wanted to shut her up by kissing her. And his mind went a little lust drunk thinking about backing her up against a wall and burying himself inside her until she could only scream his fucking name.

Yeah, you need help. He knew it. But none of that shit was going to happen. The last thing on earth he was doing was touching Jessica Jones.

———

JJ's feet hurt. Her back hurt. Her neck hurt. Hell, even her brain hurt. With a chuckle, she started to sing the song, "My neck, my back, my pussy ... " Yeah well, maybe it was better if she didn't think about her pussy and the lack of attention it was seeing these days. Her vibrator was getting a lot of airplay right now.

With Lucia only back part-time, she was having to pick up some of the slack and take over some styling duties for a couple of the fashion shows Adriana had coming.

Her specialty was makeup, but she still had a great eye, and experience doing some styling work. So Adriana was making good use of that.

But all of this extra work would be over soon. Lucia was coming back full-time in just a few weeks. And it wasn't a moment too soon. Adriana was even going to let her bring the baby to work sometimes, which made just about every woman in the office happy. Seriously, Noah and Lucia made a pretty adorable baby.

Warmth spread out through JJ's body when she thought about Isabella. God, she loved that kid. All chubby cheeks and baby belly and cute toes. *One day you'll have one.* Ha. Her subconscious thought it was a comedian. She was never keeping a guy long enough to even think about kids.

She had left work heading towards the penthouse and considered getting a cab, but it was a nice night and she needed fresh air before she was locked in.

She loved living there. She loved being mere steps away from her best friend. But what she didn't love were the constant, watchful eyes. And she understood that after some past events and the attempted kidnapping, it was for her own safety. Apparently having friends like Noah and the boys was a dangerous proposition. So she now lived in a fabulous penthouse rent-free. Unfortunately, that came with a slew of big-brother types. Seriously overprotective big-brother types. And one best friend and the most adorable baby on the planet. So she couldn't really complain about that.

But there were nights where she just needed time alone, for the love of Christ. And even though her feet hurt, she liked walking in the city at night. The hustle and bustle of the day quieted to an excited buzz for the evening.

The local bars were hopping for a Wednesday, filled with people who wanted to catch up with friends over dinner and drinks. As she passed a few, she could see couples sitting close together, heads bent towards each other or holding hands.

Would that ever be her? Not that she cared about any of that stuff. She wasn't interested in holding some guy's hand as they strolled around Central Park. Boring. She wasn't really a family and baby sort of person.

Except, you are.

Okay, fine. She was slightly green with envy whenever she saw Noah and Lucia together. And then with the baby. That was the icing on the jealousy cake. And it wasn't real jealousy. It was more of a could-she-ever-have-that-herself? kind of pang. She knew the answer to that already.

No.

And she wasn't hiding from her past. But every time she got close to someone, the nightmares would start, and she remembered what it was like to trust someone who did nothing but hurt her day after day. And she wasn't interested in that any more.

So she'd dated a slew of guys that were never, ever going to go anywhere. She'd even dated a couple of guys that tried to go somewhere. Hell, one had actually proposed, and there was one she thought she might care about. But she couldn't love any of them. Every single one of them left her cold. Well, they left her bed warm for a moment or two, but after that she didn't really want to be with them.

Because none of them gets your blood pumping like Jonas does.

Dammit. She'd promised herself she wasn't going to think

about him right now. Although maybe that's just what she needed. A fight with him, and then ten minutes of battery-operated boyfriend, and she'd be out of her little funk. Actually, that didn't sound like a bad idea.

Yeah, she was pathetic. But she had to take her pleasure somewhere. As she passed an empty boutique with the mannequin lit in the storefront window, the hairs on the back of her neck stood. JJ frowned, swearing she saw a shadow in the window, but when she turned around to look there was nobody there. Across the street a couple kissed. The guy picked the girl up and she kicked her feet out like a movie picture poster. It was cute. *And not for you.*

Still unable to shake her unease, she considered a cab but opted against it. She'd be at the penthouse soon. But she did start walking faster. When she rounded the corner at the next street, she heard footsteps tracking hers, moving at the same fast clip. A shiver ran up her spine.

She looked around again, and there was no one there, but a shadow slipped around the corner behind her. "Listen asshole, you should know I have a Taser. *And* a dick. You're going to be very unhappy if you try to do anything to me." She reached in her purse for some kind of weapon, but all she came up with was ... Oh, hell. Her vibrator.

Well, technically Lucia's. Lucia had gotten it as a gag gift a while ago, but she'd been too scared to actually use it. The thing was HUGE! And purple. Honestly, no one's vagina could accommodate that monster.

She'd tossed it in her cavernous purse the day before the fire and had never taken the thing out. Well now it was her weapon, and hey, look at that. It was actually a dick, so that part was true. Maybe she could get Matthias to rig it as some kind of Taser too.

While it might do the trick to get her off—hey, sometimes she needed to take the Jonas edge off—it was not gonna do much against a would be attacker.

What was she gonna do, orgasm him to death? *La petite mort indeed.* Fuck it, she was ready for this asshole.

But there was no one there.

Jesus, she was losing it. She turned back to head to the penthouse, and stopped short, even as the knot of fear lodged in her throat.

She thought she recognized the car that had pulled up on the corner across the street, as well as the man driving it. This meant trouble. She only had one choice: run faster.

CHAPTER FOUR

She wanted to give him a heart attack.

As Jonas raced through the streets, his eyes went back to his phone again and again to follow the tracker Matthias had sent. A blinking red dot that represented the one woman who could crawl under his skin.

He turned at the next street and gunned the engine. Luckily he'd been close, so the crazy woman hadn't been walking alone for too long. She was determined to send them all into heart failure. What the hell was she thinking walking home this late by herself?

An open parking space ahead beckoned and Jonas almost took out a part of the curb as he swung into it. He jumped out and slammed the door behind him, locking the vehicle with his key fob. He'd deliberately aimed for a street ahead of her so he could intercept her. Not that she'd appreciate his forethought at all. No. He fully expected to get an earful and a sassy string of expletives from the always delightful Jessica Jones.

He didn't have to wait long. She was about ten feet away and still hadn't noticed him, another thing he'd be sure to spank her ass for later. Hadn't he taught her the importance of being aware of your surroundings? But JJ was in a world of her own, her hips swinging as she strode down the street. It was only as she got closer and he saw her face that he realized this wasn't just JJ flouting the rules for fun. Her eyes were wild and darted around her frantically. She was clutching her bag to her side, not so much like she was afraid someone would steal it, but like she just needed to hold on to something.

She wasn't breaking the rules. She was scared. Something had sent her running, and Jonas needed to know what it was.

Jonas didn't move so she almost crashed into him.

"Watch it, asshole!"

He grabbed her arm and they struggled for a moment. "JJ, calm down. It's me."

Her eyes locked onto him, and for a moment she looked so vulnerable that it broke his heart. "Baby girl, it's me. Matthias sent me your coordinates when he saw you leave work without an escort."

She nodded frantically then glanced behind her. "I had to go. I just needed to get out of there."

"Okay, well, we can go wherever you need to."

His words, meant to calm, seemed to enrage her. She pointed her finger at him, getting annoyingly close to his eyes.

"I know I can go where I need to. That's what I'm doing. I don't need a man to tell me where I can go. Nobody controls me!"

Jonas threw up his hands. "No one said you couldn't. I'm trying to help you. Do you know how reckless this was, walking out alone? Anything could have happened to you, crazy woman!"

JJ clutched her bag tighter. "I've walked home plenty of times by myself before."

"I don't think you need me to tell you that things are different now."

The words took the wind out of her sails. JJ sagged a little, her eyes meeting his directly.

"Yeah. I know."

He fell into step beside her, happy when she followed him back to where he'd parked the car. Their usual routine was for one of the guys to escort her home from the office. If she needed to stay late, like she had tonight, she would call them when she was ready to go and someone would pick her up. Ever since everything had gone down last year, when her best friend had been stalked, JJ had seemed to understand how serious this all was and had cooperated with their efforts to keep her protected.

What had happened tonight to change that? Jonas wasn't sure what was going on but there had to have been something to send her fleeing into the night looking as haunted as she had earlier.

He held the door open for her and waited as she climbed up into the vehicle. She settled her bag on her lap and then turned to grab the seatbelt. When she saw him still standing in the doorway to the car, she hesitated.

"Is everything okay?"

"Do I look okay to you?" When she recoiled at his harsh tone, Jonas took a deep breath. "Sorry. No. I'm not okay. Not at all."

Jonas didn't offer any other explanation, just shut the door and walked around to the driver's side. Let her stew on that. Maybe then she'd see what it felt like to be left out in the dark, wondering what the hell was going on.

Right before he reached the driver's side door, he stopped. He was angry. Not just annoyed or peeved, but truly angry. Because whatever had scared JJ badly enough to have her running out without a word to her security was something that she hadn't come to him about. That didn't feel right at all. As much as they bickered, did JJ really not know that he'd drop whatever he was doing to help her?

He took a deep breath before opening the door and getting behind the wheel. JJ looked over at him. What he was feeling must have been broadcast on his face because she groaned.

"I don't want to hear the lecture right now, okay? I was busy at work and just felt like going home without calling out the cavalry, okay?"

Jonas shook his head, unbelievably disappointed. Not just because she wasn't taking her own safety seriously but also at the boldfaced lie. Did she really think he was that unobservant? It was an insult to him, not just as a security agent but as a man. He saw everything about her. She loved Lucia like a sister and put up with her best friend's fussing, even though she hated to be hovered over. She liked to watch Oskar lifting weights, much to Jonas's annoyance and jealousy.

He knew that she had a serious love affair with vodka. She had a hate affair with men and always chose badly. Including the dipshits she dated who didn't even bother to pick her up at home.

So why would she think he wouldn't see through such an obvious lie?

"I'm not going to give you a lecture, JJ. Just a reminder. If shit goes bad, we can't help you if we don't know where you are."

Jonas had expected her to have a scathing response or to tell him where to stick it. But what JJ did next was the absolute last thing he'd ever expected. She turned to him with big blue eyes.

And burst into tears.

———

JJ had been only seven when she first discovered the power of tears.

She'd gotten caught by her father sneaking a cookie. Her dad was a stickler for the no-sweets-before-dinner rule. Sneaking a cookie without asking was grounds for losing her television privileges. The moment her eyes had filled with tears, her father had started to shift on his feet. She'd added a sniffle and before she knew it, he was shoving a cookie at her.

She'd learned it applied to men in general when she'd tried it on her first boyfriend at the age of twelve, Sal Morini. Sal had tried to break up with her before the seventh grade dance so he could go out with a girl who'd put out. Namely Vicki Dematto. As soon as she'd turned on the tears, he'd backtracked. Of course at the dance she'd ditched him to party with Lucia and her friends, then told Vicci Dematto what he'd said. No girl had gone out with Sal the rest of the year.

Those early experiences had been eye-opening experiences and led to an epiphany for JJ. Ever since, she'd never had an issue using her big blue eyes to get her out of trouble.

But this time, she wasn't pulling a sympathy card or being manipulative at all. She was honestly just overwhelmed.

And furious that Jonas was the one to witness it.

But, he didn't seem to be enjoying it any more than she was. He stared at her in shock before swinging his eyes back to the road.

"Oh God, I'm sorry. I wasn't trying to yell at you."

Hearing him backtracking somehow only made it worse. She was a strong, independent woman and she didn't need to be pandered to. It was humiliating that she was crying right now when all she wanted to do was rage, but after being so sure that someone was following her, her emotions were raw and right at the surface.

"I'm not crying about that. Damn it, why am I crying at all?" She swiped at her cheeks and glared at him, as if the tears were his fault.

Although maybe they were partially his fault. She'd been holding it together while walking on her own. Then Jonas had to show up looking all kinds of edible and reminding her how much her safety meant to everyone else. Of course she'd broken down! What woman wouldn't, after a guilt trip like that?

Never mind that what he'd said wasn't even that bad. JJ needed someone to blame just then, and Jonas was readily available.

"You show up talking about Lucia and my safety. I thought someone was following me, so I told him I had a Taser and a dick, but really, all I had was the dick and I was scared, because even if that dick is huge, I mean it's probably more effective as a club."

Jonas glanced at her from the corner of his eye, and then mouthed the word *dick* slowly. Under any other circumstances JJ would have laughed. He had the cautious expression you use when talking to someone who is completely batshit crazy.

Maybe she had lost it. She reached back into her purse and pulled it out. "See, I have a legitimate dick."

His eyes went wide. "Damn, I think that thing is setting some unrealistic expectations."

She rolled her eyes. "It's not for me to use, asshole. It was a gag gift that Lucia gave back. And it was all I had as a weapon."

He worked hard to wipe the smirk off his face. "Jessica, I apologize if I made you feel like I was coming down hard on you. I just want you to know that your safety is our top priority."

He made another turn that had her shifting slightly, almost falling into the door. Part of her wanted to give him shit for his driving, but she couldn't even muster the energy. She'd been running on pure adrenaline before, but now that she was tucked into the safe confines of the car with Jonas, the fear from before came back full force. What the hell had that been about? She'd heard something; there was no way she'd imagined that. And if she'd heard something, and someone had been there, why hadn't they answered when she called out? Why would anyone want to scare her?

She ignored the voice in the back of her head. *You know who might.*

No. That was her old life. Things were different now. *Are you sure? Because maybe the fire wasn't an accident.*

She couldn't go down that spiral again. She had a brand new life now.

They pulled into the underground garage in the Blake Security building. JJ had been so deep in her thoughts that she hadn't even realized they were home. *Home.* The place you were supposed to feel safe. JJ hadn't felt like that about any place in a long time. But she could honestly acknowledge that she'd felt like that the past few months living with Lucia and her crew. Her living arrangements had seemed like a gross overreaction to her friend's security issues the prior year, but she'd soon come to love it. Surrounded by muscular, hot men all the time and living rent free. Not a bad deal at all.

But now she could see that she'd allowed it to lull her into a false sense of security. Sure she was safer living with the Blake Security team, but she must never let herself think she was truly safe. No matter where she went, she would never be safe.

"You know you can come to me with anything, right?"

JJ looked over to see that Jonas had cut the car off and turned in his seat so he could watch her. Suddenly self-conscious, she pushed her hair behind her ear.

"Sure. I mean, it's your job."

"No. Not just because it's my job."

Awareness blossomed and JJ flushed. His eyes didn't leave hers. She fidgeted with the strap of her bag, unsure how to handle this side of him. It was weird to have him looking at her like this and being nice to her. Angry and argumentative Jonas? She could handle him with one hand tied behind her back. But tender, sex-on-a-stick Jonas? Well, she didn't have the first clue as to how to act. What if she admitted that she'd wanted to call him earlier? What if she told him that she thought of him when she was alone in her bed at night and he laughed?

She'd die instantly.

"Well, I'm fine," she protested weakly. "I don't need anyone's help."

"Maybe not, but I do."

"You need my help," JJ replied, deliberately misunderstanding him.

She could tell by the flare of heat in his eyes that he was gearing up for one of their knock down, drag out wars of words. Her body responded in kind. For the first time, she catalogued the symptoms like an outsider. Increased heart rate and breathing. Flushed skin and a sense of anticipation.

God. It was so obvious looking back on it now. The whole time they'd been fighting they'd been engaging in foreplay. She could only wonder if it was as obvious to everyone else in the house. Probably. Which was just great. How was she supposed to look the others in the eye now?

"I need you to want my help. I need to help you. Because the idea of anyone fucking with you makes me crazy."

The idea that Jonas would unleash his rage on someone just because they'd bothered her pleased her greatly. She clamped down on the response. It was far too close to a "girlfriend" type of thing, and way too possessive for her taste. She'd had more than enough of possessive men who thought they owned her.

"What did I just say? Something just made the light go out of your eyes."

She shook her head. "Nothing. But I don't want anyone getting hurt because of me. I just want to be left alone."

"Who isn't allowing you to be left alone?"

Damn him for being so smart. The only way to keep from giving him all the clues he needed was to distract him. Luckily, she knew the perfect way to do that.

"Right now the only one annoying me is you. So I guess I'll say thanks for the ride and good night."

Before he could react, she reached over the console and

grabbed the front of his shirt. He let her tug him until he was close enough for her to smell the scent of his cologne. Their eyes met, and suddenly Jonas smiled. The impact of it, especially so close, made JJ feel like she was flying. And suddenly this wasn't about distracting him anymore. It was about doing what she'd wanted to do for ages.

Kiss him.

His lips softened under hers and he let out a soft groan that ricocheted through the still interior of the car. It was incredibly intimate, secluded there with just the two of them and the rapidly increasing sound of their breathing. For those moments, they weren't Jonas and JJ, mortal enemies.

They were two people who connected like lightning, taking each other in like they wanted to merge into one being.

She gasped and a moan slipped loose. Jonas took that opportunity to slip his hand into her hair, anchor her head, and deepen the kiss, his tongue sliding over hers expertly.

JJ hooked her arm around his neck, holding him still, and he opened his mouth wider like he was trying to swallow her whole. If the console hadn't been between them, she likely would have climbed into his lap, but instead she just sucked on his lower lip until he moaned into her mouth, the sound finally bringing her back to reality.

They stayed for a beat staring at each other before she pulled back and opened the door. The rush of cool air coming in cleared her head, and JJ wondered if it had finally happened. After years of pretending to be okay, if maybe she'd finally had a mental breakdown.

"JJ, what just—"

"Good night, Jonas." She closed the door and walked quickly to the elevator.

For the first time that day, luck was on her side, because after she leaned forward for the retinal scan, the doors opened immediately.

The doors closed just as Jonas rushed up. She heard his muffled curse get fainter as the elevator ascended.

"Good night, indeed." JJ touched her mouth.

CHAPTER FIVE

O f all the mistakes he'd ever made in his life that had to be the dumbest one. *Kissing Jessica Jones.* Because now there was no way he was ever getting the taste of her out of his system. Jonas followed behind JJ, watching her ass sashay back and forth as she headed straight for her room. Aching all over, he went straight for the conference room. He'd left his laptop and needed to collect a few things before he headed home.

What had he been thinking? The problem was that now that he'd tasted her, it was all he could think about. Even before the sweet, scorching slide of her lips over his, he'd already been a little too obsessed with her. Because while she might seem innocuous, she was sly, working her way under his skin for the sheer pleasure of torturing him to death.

Fuck, he was losing it. He needed to get his shit and then to put some distance between the two of them. He just had to put her out of his mind. It would be fine. He was a master of control.

Not with her you're not.

Under penalty of death, he would never admit just how often he thought about JJ. That would only stroke her ego … amongst other things. His perverted mind had all kinds of ideas about what the hell else of hers he could stroke.

No. Not gonna go there.

He'd lost count of how many times he'd had a little shower workout just thinking about her lips. Or that sexy smile, or the way her ass filled out her jeans.

Nope. Not going to happen. Ever. And it wasn't that he was obsessed with her exactly, it was more that she challenged him. Irritated him. Sometimes he just wanted to kiss that smug smile right off her face.

Well, how did that feel?

Fucking incredible. The best tasting chocolate ice cream

of his life topped with something even more decadent. JJ's lips topped his *Never Touch* list.

He shook his head. Why did he do it?

You really want to answer that?

He ignored that thought. He didn't even *like* her. She was bossy, irritating, loud ... Fuck, was she fucking loud.

Well, lucky for you, you now have a way to shut her up.

And did he ever. He just kept thinking of the way she'd stared at him. Lips parted on a gasp, looking soft and mussed, right before he'd slipped his hand in her hair, anchored her head, and then deepened the kiss. Now her taste haunted him as it followed him around like a wraith.

Shit.

This wasn't helping. Because, what do you know, he was getting a boner. Fan-fucking-tastic. He stormed into the conference room and slammed the door behind him, even though the door didn't exactly slam since it was on soft hinges.

He dropped his ass into one of the cushioned seats and scowled at his laptop. He quickly checked his emails while he willed his dick to lay down.

Damn it.

She was not supposed to affect him like this. Where was some of that infamous control?

Oh yeah? That control you displayed with Mira the other night? How about the control you displayed with Clint?

Shit. Lately it was like he was walking on a tightrope and any little thing would set him on edge. Send him over.

Kissing JJ certainly had him teetering and clamoring to get himself back on steady footing.

They could forget this. Pretend it never happened. Pretend that she didn't taste like sin and sex and temptation all rolled into one. He could forget. It was fine. Everything was just fucking *fine.* All he had to do was completely forget that soft moaning sound she made when he slid his tongue into her mouth. It was easy.

Dick, *still* hard. "Little note, asshole, you are not doing me any favors right now," he mumbled to his dick. The damn thing didn't care. It just continued to twitch in his pants as if to say, "I know she's over here somewhere; why don't we go finish that kiss?"

The hell he was going to do that. He was never touching her again.

"So, how was it?"

Jonas snapped his head up and met gazes with Oskar Mueller. After Matthias, Oskar was the most senior member of Blake Security. He and Noah had crossed paths in Noah's old life as an assassin. When he started Blake Security, he called Oskar. The German was one of the best forensic accountants in the business. And also a general badass with a penchant for knocking skulls.

Jonas's first thought was to say 'fucking incredible. She tastes like you think she would taste.' But no, he wasn't an idiot. Oskar liked to gossip more than any high school girl Jonas had ever seen. So instead, Jonas frowned and asked for clarification. "What do you mean?"

Oskar shrugged. "Blondie rolled in on a tear. Obviously she's pissed about something. Gotta tell you, I'm sorry I missed that fight. You two bickering is often the highlight of my day."

"You're an asshole."

"Yep, doesn't change the fact I'd like to see that fight. One of these days, I'm telling you it's gonna go all Mayweather and Pacquiao and I want a ringside seat."

"It was fine. She was JJ, as usual."

Oskar shook his head. "What the hell was she doing walking on her own anyway?"

Jonas buried the flare of anger at what could have happened to her. "I have no idea why that woman does anything. She's a complete mystery. She makes no flipping sense. Makes her even more infuriating."

"Tell me about it. If I didn't know better, I'd swear she does some of the stuff she does so we'll notice and come along and save her. But that also doesn't jive because she doesn't have a martyr complex. That chick is tough as nails and scares me a little."

Jonas snorted. "As she should. You never know what arsenal of weapons she's hiding." Except now Jonas sort of had an idea. Her lips needed to be classified as certified lethal weapons. And he had a feeling that sooner or later, she'd be using them to take him out.

———

The first stop JJ made was the nursery, because she knew that's exactly where she would find Lucia. And after the crazy that had just happened in the car with Jonas, she needed her best friend, pronto.

Lucia looked up with a smile. "Hey, I was just feeding the baby. Wanna hold her when I'm done?"

JJ nodded absently and sank down into the soft lounger that had been placed in the corner of the nursery, and Lucia raised a brow. "What's the matter?"

How was she supposed to answer that exactly?

Jonas Castillo just made my toes curl with a simple kiss?

That was the core of what was bothering her. It wasn't like he busted out any magic tricks or anything like that. It had been a simple kiss, but it had rocked her to her core.

Her whole damn body felt like it was vibrating. This was Jonas. She didn't like Jonas. Moreover, Jonas didn't like her.

So why did that kiss just rock your world?

JJ groaned and covered her face with her hands. "So, you know how sometimes we make a stupid choice, and then have to pay the consequences?"

Lucia laughed. "Did you *accidentally* set Jonas's closet on fire?" Lucia used the word accidentally with air quotes.

"No. I didn't. But I should've. Now you're giving me ideas."

Her friend laughed. "Oh no. Just don't tell him I gave you that one. You know how that man is about his clothes and shoes."

"You know, I can't even get excited about that right now I'm so upset."

Lucia sat forward. "What's wrong? Do we need to get —"

JJ held up a hand. She knew exactly what Lucia was going to say. Get Noah in here; get the whole squad to go beat down whoever the hell had pissed her off. While JJ did like having an ass-kicking team behind her, they were very unlikely to kick the ass of one of their own. "No. This doesn't need to involve Noah or anyone else for that matter."

Her bestie frowned. "What's going on?"

"What's going on is Jonas kissed me." JJ sat back and waited for Lucia to process that bombshell.

But nothing.

Her best friend didn't even raise a brow, purse a lip, or let her mouth hang open. None of that. "Did you not hear me? Jonas *kissed* me. I mean, yes I kissed him first but that was just to shut him up. I wasn't expecting him to kiss me back."

Lucia shrugged. "Well, it's about time. My only concern is somehow you don't look at all happy about it, or satisfied." She leaned forward. "Oh my God, is he bad at it?"

JJ just blinked at her. "Are you serious right now? I'm telling you this catastrophic event happened and you're sitting there like you expected it to?"

Lucia shrugged. "Yeah. Because you two have been snapping around each other for ages. It's time you guys finally got the ball rolling. So if it wasn't bad, then what's your problem?"

"This is *Jonas*. My nemesis, remember."

Lucia giggled. "He's hardly your nemesis. He just likes to push your buttons and vice versa." Isabella stopped nursing and whacked her mother's breast with a tiny fist to let her know that she was done. When Lucia adjusted her clothing, she held the little tiny bundle out to JJ. "You want to hold her?"

That was hardly fair. Lucia was plying her with adorable baby mojo. Still though, JJ rose and took her little niece. "Hi, Angel. Maybe you'll be appropriately horrified by the fact that Jonas and I kissed."

But apparently Isabella was just as big a traitor as her

mother was. She just gave JJ a happy baby smile and burped.

"Well, fat lot of good you are for advice."

Lucia laughed. "What did you expect? She's a baby. Okay, let me get my bestie hat on." Lucia took several deep breaths and closed her eyes, and when she opened them again she slapped her cheeks. "Oh my God, you and Jonas kissed? What happened?"

JJ couldn't help the smile that tugged at her lips. "Now *that* is the appropriate reaction." JJ eased down on the couch, holding Isabella as she started to fall asleep. "Okay, so I was leaving work and I decided I wanted to walk."

Already Lucia was frowning. JJ rushed to explain. "I know. I should've just taken a taxi. But you know, I've been feeling like I've been locked up in this penthouse. And I just needed a night, hell, even like thirty minutes, to myself. Is that so wrong? And before you answer that, just think about how you would feel if you were me."

Lucia opened her mouth to say something, but then snapped it shut. JJ continued. "I don't know how he found out, but before I knew it, Jonas was there, yelling at me, insisting I get in the car. Can you imagine? I'm a grown woman. I can walk if I want to."

"But it's not safe, JJ," Lucia said.

"Sometimes don't you think the security protocols are a little too much? You, of all people, should understand that."

Lucia sighed. "Okay, you have a point. So what happened then?"

"So, we're doing the usual thing, you know, fighting. Me threatening to relieve him of his balls."

"Yeah, pretty much like any other day."

JJ had gone over that span of five minutes in the car a dozen times already. Like a reel in her head over, and over, and over again, she could pinpoint when something had changed, when the need shifted.

That moment when all she could concentrate on was the feel of Jonas's firm lips on hers, his tongue sliding into her mouth. The way his hand fisted in her hair, and the way he moaned when she whimpered. Like she was the best tasting ice cream on a hot summer's day.

"I don't know what happened. But once again I was shouting at him and explaining to him how I could take care of myself. The next thing I know we're kissing. And the worst thing is, it was like a toe-curling, slap-your-last-boyfriend-for-kissing-you-shitty kind of kiss. I mean, the man knows what he's doing. If you ever tell him that, I will kill you."

Baby Isabella just gurgled and kicked her feet, and then sighed before promptly closing her eyes. *Oh yeah. Real helpful.*

Lucia shook her head. "That doesn't even sound like Jonas. I mean, were you goading him?"

JJ laughed. "This is me. I'm *always* goading him. So how was this time any different from any other time?"

"Maybe it was the straw that broke the camel's back. And you guys have been circling each other forever. Maybe he snapped."

"Maybe. What does this mean? Because as quickly as it started, it was over all too soon. I mean, how is the man gonna just give me a taste? It's like he knows it's been too long since I've been laid, and he's devised a new way to torture me. I don't know what to do. Help me."

"You're asking me, but you're not going to like my answer," Lucia said. "But maybe you just talk to him. For once, try not to snap at each other. For once, just acknowledge that you two have the hots and move from there."

JJ frowned. "You're right. I don't like that answer."

Lucia laughed. "So what are you going to do? It's not like you can avoid him. It's not like you can pretend this didn't happen. Or that you didn't like it."

And therein lay the rub. She *had* liked it. *A lot.* Matter-of-fact, she liked it so much she wanted to rub her whole body all over him. Hell, she'd arched into that kiss, practically begging him to keep touching her. And she had no idea what she was going to do about that.

Because no way in hell could she do it again.

CHAPTER SIX

Jonas held out a hand to assist his client out of the car. Normally he enjoyed these out of town jobs but not today. He glanced around them, edgy as fuck and not sure exactly why. His assignment was to keep Lindsey Meyers and her son safe and out of sight while Noah dealt with her ex-husband. This was nothing he hadn't done before.

"Thank you," Lindsey whispered, clutching her duffel bag to her chest as she climbed down. Immediately, she moved to the back of the car to get her son, Henry, out of his booster seat.

Lindsey had been living in Atlanta for the past year after divorcing her husband. Too bad the asshole hadn't gotten the point.

He sighed. Goddamn he was tired. He would never make fun of Ryan for dodging these types of cases again. Domestic calls were so draining. It was exhausting trying to help people who weren't ready to help themselves.

"Okay, so I've booked us into two rooms here under a false name. No one will find you here. Our rooms have an adjoining door. Please leave it unlocked so I can get to you quickly if you should need me."

Lindsey nodded that she understood. "Thank you. I feel bad that you have to be away from home just to babysit me."

Jonas smiled, trying to put her at ease. That was one of the most common things they heard from their female clients. Women who'd been so conditioned not to make waves that they apologized constantly for trouble that wasn't of their own making.

"There's no reason for you to feel bad. It's my job. Also, I'm pretty sure Noah is going to enjoy intimidating your ex-husband while we're here. So put on a movie, get comfortable. If you want to order takeout, let me know and I'll have them bring it my room first."

"Okay. I can do that." Lindsey pushed her hair behind her

ear nervously, but she looked slightly less scared than when they arrived.

Henry held tight to her hand, peering up at Jonas suspiciously. He'd never spent much time around kids this age, but Jonas supposed he would have been suspicious too if some guy he'd never seen was driving him around.

Jonas led them to the front desk where he picked up the keys to their rooms. Matthias had checked them in remotely, so after retrieving the key, they took the elevator up to the tenth floor.

"Do you have a girlfriend?" Lindsey asked curiously.

Jonas froze. "No time for that. Love is too much work."

The elevator stopped at their floor, and he wasted no time escorting them off. It wasn't unusual for clients to ask about his personal life. Spending so much time with someone, often having your life literally in their hands, forged bonds that felt intimate. Most people wanted to know more about the person protecting them.

Only he'd found that when the clients doing the asking were young, attractive women, it could lead to uncomfortable situations and misunderstandings. So he tried to remain a mystery.

"Here we go. Room 1014." He swiped the key and they were in. "Wait here."

Lindsey waited by the door obediently, clutching Henry's hand tightly while Jonas checked out every inch of the suite. The door to his room next door was standing open, as he'd requested. That room was empty, too. He came back to find them still standing next to the front door.

"It's okay. You can go ahead and relax now. I'll check in with the team and keep you updated."

Lindsey's sigh of relief was the best thank you he could have received.

She smiled at him. "You're really good at this."

"I hope so. I'm not much good at anything else."

His joke made her smile. "You're a nice guy. I hope you do find time for love one day, and that you don't let all the bad relationships you see scare you away. Love isn't supposed to be hard. It took me a long time to see that."

Jonas nodded politely and then walked through the connecting door into his room. He'd already dropped his own overnight bag on the bed, but he wouldn't be sleeping. Noah would be calling with an update soon, and he needed to be ready.

With so much time to fill, his brain inevitably went to the one thing he'd been trying to ignore all day.

JJ.

He sat on the edge of the bed and scrubbed his hands over his face. He'd been trying not to think of her. But trying not to think of her was like trying not to breathe. She was in him, deep, completely entwined with his every thought and function. That kiss, that fucking kiss, replayed over and over on a loop in the back of his mind constantly.

What the hell had he been thinking?

Not that he would take all the blame. Oh no, part of the responsibility for this clusterfuck rested solidly on JJ's shoulders. She'd pulled him in, knowing what her tempting mouth did to him. He shook his head. She'd just been playing around like they always did. She'd kissed him on the cheek before. When she did it he was always worried she'd follow through on the threat in her eyes and bite a hole in his cheek.

But this time the crafty little vixen had gotten a little more than she'd expected. Jonas grunted, thinking of the shocked, furious, and aroused look on her face once she'd finally pulled back. It was a miracle she hadn't slugged him. Honestly, he wasn't sure if she even understood why she hadn't. But he knew all too well what this kind of desire led to. It was dangerous and all-consuming, the kind that made smart men give up their careers and risk their lives.

A knock on the door drew him from his thoughts. He sprang up just as Lindsey stuck her head in.

"Everything okay?" he asked.

She held up the room service menu. "Yeah, but Henry will be hungry soon. I figured we'd better put our order in now. Should I order something for you, too?"

Jonas accepted the menu she held out, and then pointed to the only thing on there that looked like a burger.

"Use my phone," he instructed and then moved back so she could reach it. He wasn't even hungry, just grateful for the interruption. Lindsey was a reminder of all the reasons he had to stay away from JJ. Relationships were a minefield, even when the two parties started off on solid ground.

With a past like his, Jonas wasn't the right guy for anyone to bet on. But it didn't mean that he couldn't look out for her.

He would do what he did best: take care of her from afar.

———

JJ caught herself twisting the hem of her loose top and clenched her fingers into a fist. It was a little after seven o'clock, and she should have been well on her way home by now. Instead she was reviewing some last minute layouts for a magazine spread and waiting to meet one of the volunteers from Hope Springs.

JJ gulped. This was really happening.

It shouldn't be that big of a deal, really. This was no different than any of the other charity events she'd worked on.

Bullshit.

JJ ignored the uneasy feeling that crept up the back of her neck. There was no use pretending this wasn't a big deal. Very soon a woman was going to walk in here with a story that was all too familiar. Someone who understood, just as she did, how important appearances were to rebuilding your life. Wasn't that part of why JJ had been attracted to makeup? She'd always loved how transforming her appearance could give her a confidence boost. It was only later that she'd learned how transforming her appearance could hide the evidence of her private hell.

A whisper outside her office door drew her attention.

"It's okay, you can come right in!" JJ called.

She frantically tried to clear her desk, pulling all the papers and magazines into a neat pile on the right side. There was always someone staying late at the office. Adriana liked to work her people to the bone and there was never any shortage of things to do, especially as they drew closer to fashion week. But despite how busy the office always was, JJ knew how intimidating it could be to ask anyone for help or directions.

She stood and stepped over the box of sample clothing on the floor. Damn, she needed to clean this place up. Her office was the size of a shoebox anyway, so it really couldn't stand any clutter. Once clear of the debris on the floor, she stuck her head around the doorjamb and into the hallway.

The empty hallway.

Puzzled, she glanced both ways. She'd definitely heard someone out here. Behind her, the phone on her desk rang. JJ walked back over to her desk and snatched the receiver.

"Hello?"

There was nothing but silence but she could hear that the line was open. A hush, like someone trying not to breathe too hard.

"Hello? Who is this?" JJ demanded, creeped out and beyond angry about it. The skin on her arms prickled and she shivered, and JJ was suddenly feeling very exposed and alone, being in the office so late.

She hung up the phone and rubbed the goose bumps standing up on her arms. Her office was bordered by windows on one side, and when she'd first gotten the job, that had seemed like a perk. But now, standing in the office alone, JJ felt like she was inside a fishbowl, on display to anyone who might be watching from one of the surrounding buildings.

A knock on the door startled her, and she spun around. The young woman in the doorway took a hesitant step back at JJ's no-doubt feral expression.

"Sorry! I'm here from Hope Springs. The guy at the front said I could come straight back."

"Of course. Come right in." JJ swallowed the rush of embarrassment at being caught freaking herself out in the middle of an empty office. What the hell was wrong with her?

Luckily the young woman, a studious type named Alison, didn't seem to mind her distraction. Before long, despite her earlier hesitation, JJ found herself completely immersed in the young woman's description of their new job program.

"This is going to help so many women," Alison concluded. "Thank you for agreeing to help. Some people don't understand the confidence boost that just looking better can give you. Especially when you've been made to feel that dressing up is flirting. That was always a trigger for my ex. Any time I wore makeup, he assumed I was using it to flirt with other men."

JJ's hand clenched, crumpling the paper she was holding. "That's so familiar. Everything becomes your fault. Until finally, you're afraid of your own shadow and can barely look anyone in the eye."

"Yes. That's it exactly." Alison smiled at her sadly. "Sounds like you understand all too well."

That jarred JJ out of her languid state. She'd been so

caught up in Alison's descriptions of the program and all the great things they were doing that she'd forgotten where she was and who she was talking to. It was alarming that she could forget so easily. Especially when she'd spent years burying that part of her life so deep that no one could ever find out.

"Well, I can't even imagine what you've been through. But I want to help however I can." JJ stood and held out her hand, hoping that would signal that the meeting was over without being rude.

Alison shook her hand with a knowing look. "I'll be in touch about the dates for the makeup seminars. Also, we'll send a volunteer over to pick up the clothes Adriana agreed to donate next week."

JJ hoped she was nodding in the right places and saying the right things. Her head spun a little as a sudden wave of dizziness hit her. No, she did not have time for this nonsense. She refused to get a migraine right now.

But as her panic increased, so did the throbbing behind her eyes. Oh, God no, not right now, she thought. Migraines loved to sneak up on her whenever possible, but she didn't have her medication with her. She closed her eyes briefly and took a deep breath. It was all this stress with no outlet. Of course it was building up. Stress was a huge migraine trigger for her and always had been.

She hated it. Hated the weakness of it and how it rendered her completely vulnerable. For years, she'd taken increasingly stronger medication, hoping to find something that could cure her, but it turned out her migraines were something that had to be managed. By avoiding stress, eating well, exercising, and avoiding triggers.

JJ sighed in relief as Alison finally walked out. She rubbed at her temples with the pads of her fingers. That was it. Looked like she'd be spending the night under the covers trying not to move. As she gathered her things to leave, the phone on her desk rang again. When she picked it up and heard nothing but silence, JJ wondered how she was supposed to manage her stress when the world around her was determined to throw her past in her face?

CHAPTER SEVEN

Fuck, Jonas was exhausted. After the last several days with Lindsey Myers, he was ready to get back to New York. But the work they were doing was important. And he was glad to see Lindsey settled in.

At first he hadn't wanted to come down to Atlanta to get her set up. The client was great, a sweet woman. But he internalized too much of this shit, especially when there were kids involved. He remembered people trying to help his mother. But truth be told, this little trip was a good excuse to get the hell away from New York. To get the hell away from JJ. His mind was still rattling with every-thing that had happened right before he left. *Go on, say it. You fucked up by kissing her.*

And yes, he'd kissed her back because his temper was up. And his curiosity had flared. And because she was driving him fucking insane. But still, he knew better. He knew that was a line that he couldn't uncross. But he'd gone ahead and crossed it anyway. What the hell was wrong with him? He shook his head to clear it and dragged his attention back to the matter at hand.

He turned to Lindsey with a smile. "Okay, so let's go over the panel one more time."

She grinned at him. "I swear you're hovering over me like a mother hen. I have the code. It's the reverse of Henry's birthday and my birthday. I won't forget those dates."

"I know. But humor me. It'll help to know that you know exactly what to do."

Though she rolled her eyes, she went straight to the panel hidden behind the painting, moved the painting aside, plugged in the code and a star. The star meant all was safe. If she plugged in the code and hit pound, that was an alert to the security company that even though she was punching in the code, she was doing it under duress. And when the company called, they would know that any response she made was again under duress; they would send the police with a quiet presence, no sirens, no lights. Jonas would rather not think about what would happen in that scenario. Because that scenario would mean that her ex-husband had found her and their son Henry. It would mean that he had failed her.

Noah and Dylan had tracked the guy down, and lo and behold, he'd had drugs on him, which was a violation of his parole. So it was back to prison for the fidiot. But the jackhole had friends. Too many low-life friends.

Which is why Noah and the crew had to work to get her as far away from him as possible. She'd left without any money and just the clothes on her back. Noah had a slush fund for such occasions, as well as safe houses in several cities across the country. Blake Security had rented her the house for next to nothing and she could stay as long as she wanted. The only caveat was that if they had someone they needed to hide in a hurry, she put them up in the spare room until they could move whoever it was safely.

They'd also gotten her a job. A decent-paying one that would allow her to afford to send Henry to a good school. All this so she would be safe.

He nodded his approval. "Good. I'm glad you remember."

"I told you I would. Now, do you want me to get your last slice of pie before you have to head back to New York?"

"I think you already know the answer to that." He followed her into the kitchen. He liked her. And he hoped she would be able to stay safe. Unlike the last woman he'd tried to help.

———

Jonas made it to the airport and caught the last flight back from Atlanta, crammed into one of those tiny airline seats. He headed back to his apartment around seven o'clock, and the last thing he wanted to do was ever leave again. All he wanted was to grab a shower and crash. But his damn phone rang the moment he stepped foot into his place.

He scowled at it hoping that it wasn't Noah. He simply did not have the energy for some team emergency at the moment. The name on the caller ID however, was unexpected. And he answered immediately. "Mira, what's wrong? Are you okay?"

"Yes, I'm fine. I'm so sorry to call so late. But do you think that maybe we can meet for a moment? Back at the coffee shop?"

He didn't even think. All he did was walk faster to deposit his weekender bag on his bed and change out his jacket for something that would conceal his holster. "I'm on my way."

Ten minutes later, he found her at the exact same table where they'd sat the last time. When she looked up, she gave him a weak smile, and he went to join her. "Mira, I was worried. Are you okay?"

"I'm so sorry I worried you. I'm fine. Honestly."

When he just stared down at her, inspecting her for any outward bruising, she shifted uncomfortably. "Honestly. Can you please have a seat? I wanted to say something."

Jonas slid into the seat next to her. "Well, you look okay. He hasn't hurt you has he?"

She didn't even look surprised that he knew about her being back with her ex. But color did tint her cheeks. "I think you were right."

Jonas's brows snapped down. "I would rather not be right about all the things I'm thinking. Elaborate. Has he hurt you again?"

She shook her head. But her hands shook. "No. Not yet. But," she hesitated for a moment, "I can see it. The anger in him, the rage. There are flashes of it, and at the end of the day I'm still living the exact same way I was. Afraid. Afraid to do anything, afraid to talk, afraid to move, afraid to not have dinner on the table. He tells me that I don't need to do that. That the anger management worked or whatever, but I don't believe him. And so I'm afraid."

He nodded sagely. "You want Noah and I to clear him out? We'll grab the guys and swing on by to make sure he stays far away from you."

She shook her head. "I can do this on my own. "

"No one can do this on their own. " He licked his lips and wondered if he should tell her how he ended up here. Sitting across from a woman like her, one that so desperately needed help but refused to take it. And then the words were spilling out before he could even stop them. "My mother. She was the most beautiful woman I have ever seen in my life. You know when they say people have a light that shines through them? She was one of those people."

Mira frowned, as if not quite certain why Jonas was telling her the story. But she stayed quiet.

"My father, on the other hand ... Pure asshole through and through. Believed that he walked on water and everyone else should bow before him. And boy oh boy, did he have a shitty temper. It didn't even take much to set him off. A good morning not said the right way, and you'd get a quick knock across your head. He used to pick her up and haul her to the floor for not having dinner ready. You can probably imagine."

Mira nodded. "Oh, too well."

"And then there's me. He wanted me to be the best. To brag to everyone about how I was the best. And God help me if I didn't perform. He would take it out on my mother. Never me. I would beg for him to take it out on me. But always her. And she stayed. It didn't matter how many times I begged her to go; she stayed. Eventually he killed her. I don't want something like that to happen to you, Mira."

Her eyes filled with tears. And she blinked them rapidly away. "I don't want that to be me either. I thought he'd changed. I thought the anger management was working. But I think I'm still the same person. I've still been conditioned to be afraid of him. And he's still the same person. He tries to control his anger, but he's not very good at it. And I think I'm going to bear the brunt of that soon enough if I'm not careful."

"What do you need? Do you need a place to stay? We have safe houses all over the city. New Jersey, Philly. We can get you relocated. If you need money, we have a slush fund for these things. Hell, I was just making good use of it in Atlanta today. Let us help you. I don't want you going back to that house. Because he will tell you all about how he's changed and how he'll never do it again, and I'm terrified for you."

She shook her head. "No. I don't need any of that stuff. You and your team did plenty for me, and I didn't listen. I didn't take any of that advice. But I'm taking it now. My bag is in the car. I applied for a job months ago when I was first leaving him. And I interviewed, but I didn't hear back so I didn't think anything of it. But they called today, and I knew if I told him I wanted to take the job it was not going to end well. And maybe I'm not the same person, but I couldn't stand the idea of him beating me over something I was so excited and happy about. I knew I had to go. I just wanted to say thank you and good-bye before I left. I'm going to use the drive down to reflect on my life and what I really want from it. "

Some of the weight that pressed down on his chest the moment he'd met Mira Ashton eased up. "You don't have to say thank you."

"Yes, I do. I know I owe you my life. And you don't have to worry about me. I still have the papers the British guy on your team made me for my new identity. I don't have any family anyway. So I get to vanish. I just wanted you to know. And then to ask you to say thank you to Noah and the rest of your team."

He nodded his acceptance and they both stood. But before she could turn and walk away, he grabbed her hand gently. "I mean it. Mira. You need anything, anything at all, call us. You know the number by heart. We will help you. It doesn't matter what it is."

Jonas could only stand back and watch as she left, and he prayed that this time, *this time*, he was actually able to save one of them.

———

J balanced the phone to her ear even as she held two cups of coffee, had a shoulder bag containing several samples on her arm, and teetered on four-inch heels. Adriana had sent her out for a samples run, and of course, she stopped to get herself a reward coffee.

After a week of working with the Hope Springs charity,

her nerves were frayed. And her heart was broken. In so many ways, she'd come a million miles from where she'd been. She was no longer that young girl who was too scared to say anything, too concerned about what everyone would think, so worried about her life and those around her. But in other ways, she was still in the exact same spot. She wore her outer shell of bravado every morning like a set of clothes. It was her Teflon suit.

Nothing fazed her; nothing bothered her. She was a poor facsimile of the person she wanted to be. The person she knew she wasn't. So every morning when she woke up, she knew she was telling everyone a lie. Worse yet, she needed the suit. She needed it to survive on a daily basis. Working with Hope Springs just reminded her of who she'd been, of who she was, deep down inside. If that wasn't good enough to fray the nerves on a daily basis, then she didn't know what was.

And certainly, caffeine isn't going to help.

Yeah, maybe not, but coffee was one of life's little heaven-sent pleasures. So she was going to have her coffee. And then she was going to stick her nose back to the grind-stone and just power through this whole thing. She wanted to help these women. She wanted to get them to freedom. She wanted to get them safe and away from harm.

The problem was there was an inherent part of her that wanted to scream, "You will not be safe. No matter what you do, you will carry the fear with you the rest of your life." But since this was supposed to be uplifting, she didn't think that was the best course of action.

The springtime breeze with the blare of taxicabs' horns all around her made her almost able to forget. With the flow of pedestrian traffic going mostly against her, she could practically get lost in the sea of faces. She made a right turn at the corner to head back toward her office and stopped short. Across the street in Longwinds boutique, clear as day, she saw a familiar face.

Her heart rate sped up and her breathing hitched. *No. It can't be him.* She'd already convinced herself she'd hallucinated his car at the curb the other day. Her feet were rooted to the concrete as she stared for a long moment. Passersby jostled her backwards and forwards as they hurried past her on the way to wherever they were going.

But still she stared. No, this couldn't be happening. This was not her life. She didn't want this; she didn't *need* this. She was done with this part of her life wasn't she?

You'll never be done.

Oh, fuck that. She wasn't going to stand here. She didn't want to be afraid anymore. She had to be sure.

JJ darted out into the traffic between the taxicabs and horns blaring at her. But she didn't care. It's not like they were going anywhere anyway. The traffic was at a near standstill. Her heels made a clip-clop sound as she skipped over the pavement and straight to the boutique.

By the time she made it across the street, past the white wood and glass doors, she didn't see anyone. There were a couple of shoppers and one sales-woman helping someone out. What the hell? No, she hadn't imagined that. She'd seen him. He'd been here.

Or is your mind playing tricks on you? You're being forced to examine who you are. Who you've been. And the person who made you that way.

No, no, no. He couldn't be here. She hadn't seen him in so many years. Seven now? It couldn't be. She headed back for the dressing rooms, shoving aside every single curtain. Luckily there was no one back there.

Stacking her two coffees one on top of the other, she

opened the staff only doors and peered in. There was no one there. How could she have made that mistake?

"Hey, you can't be back here."

The sales girl had come around to see what she was up to. "I'm so sorry. I was looking for someone. I saw him in the mirror that you have out there. Tall, 6'3" - 6'4". Dark hair."

The sales girl shook her head. "I'm sorry. There was no one who fits that description back here."

JJ shook her head. "No. I saw him. It was him. Are you sure? I'm not crazy. It was *him*."

The sales girl's brows lifted, and she backed away a step. "I'm sorry, but I'm going to have to ask you to leave. If you don't, I will call the police."

The police. She would welcome them coming. *Except, what are you going to tell them? I saw my psycho ex. The one I never filed charges against or got a restraining order against. That ex. He was in the store. I need him found.*

No. Likely all they would do was arrest her for trespassing or something. "I'm sorry. I'll go. Are you sure—?"

The sales girl shook her head. "There is no one here except my customers."

JJ nodded. *Shit.* Maybe her mind was playing tricks on her. It was understandable, considering everything she'd been dealing with over the last week. She was seeing ghosts where there weren't any. Coffees back in hand, she stepped back out of the boutique just as her phone rang.

Again she stacked the cups while she hunted the phone out of her pocket. "Hello?"

"You always did look good in red."

JJ whirled around, searching for any familiar faces in the crowd. On the turn though, her heel caught, and her coffees tipped, fell over, and splashed everywhere. Pedestrians jumped out of the way of the scalding hot dark liquid. But JJ didn't care. She'd find him. "How'd you get my number?"

"I've *always* had your number." The low rumbling laugh on the phone was cold and icy. All too familiar. After all these years. He'd found her.

CHAPTER EIGHT

He knew the moment he heard her voice that something was wrong.

Jonas had just finished a session of lifting weights and grabbed a shower. He'd had a shitty morning and early afternoon. He figured that if he could get some gym time in, at least he'd have done something productive that day. If it were anyone else, he wouldn't have even answered the phone. But as soon as JJ's picture flashed on the screen, he dropped the weights he was putting away right where he stood.

"Hey, JJ. Everything okay?"

"Jonas! Oh my God."

Her voice came through the phone like a shriek, and the shrill sound froze him in his tracks. He'd heard her sound like a lot of things—pissed off, happy, playful and exhausted—but never terrified. His girl was tough as nails. Which made the palpable fear in her voice even more alarming.

"JJ, what's going on? Where are you right now?"

There was only harsh breathing followed by a soft sob. Jonas gripped the phone so hard it was a miracle it didn't shatter in his hand. In the span of ten seconds every terrible thing he'd ever seen in his nightmares raced through his mind.

"So help me ... JJ, tell me where you are."

"I'm on the street. Outside of Longwinds." Another sob.

Jonas was already moving. "Are you alone?"

"No ... I don't know. Jonas, *I need you.*"

Jonas could barely breathe as everything inside him clenched and his blood turned to ice. It had to be bad for her to ask for his help. Fuck. He was on the parking level now and his steps quickened as he approached his Jeep.

"JJ, I need you to keep talking to me. Let me know you're okay."

After the world's longest pause, one in which he died a thousand times over, she finally spoke. "I'm here. I'm okay. But I know there was someone."

Her voice was shaky. She was probably in shock.

If anyone had hurt her ... Why the hell hadn't he insisted on accompanying her everywhere? Considering how thoroughly she'd bewitched him, it was hardly a stretch to imagine that other men felt the same way. He'd seen what some men did to the women they claimed to love. Despite how much she hated having a security detail, he should have put his foot down and insisted. Why hadn't he taken care of her?

Noah hadn't spared any expense or left any stone unturned when it came to ensuring Lucia's safety. Why hadn't he done the same?

But Lucia and Noah are together. JJ isn't yours, the rational part of his brain argued.

The hell she isn't, he thought bitterly. She might not know it yet but she was his just as surely as he was hers. Every breath he took belonged to her.

"I'm almost there, JJ. Just hang on, okay?"

He was probably going to end up in some police chase, considering how crazy he was driving but he didn't bother slowing down. Let them chase him. As long as he got to JJ and made sure she was safe, they could put him in handcuffs. It was nothing that hadn't been done before.

The dark thought accompanied him as he raced through the streets and finally pulled up in front of Longwinds. He knew the boutique only because it was one of Lucia and JJ's favorite stores. His eyes sifted through the crowds walking on the sidewalk in front of the store until he locked onto a small shape a few yards away from the door. JJ was sitting on the hard concrete, her arms curled around her knees, her blond hair falling over her face like a shield.

He parked illegally and jumped out. JJ didn't notice him until he was right in front of her. She raised her head and stared through him, her big blue eyes glassy with unshed tears.

"I want to go home," she confessed in a small voice.

Jonas felt his heart break wide open right then and there.

"Come on, baby. Let's get you off the ground."

The sense of wrongness amplified when she didn't fight him, instead wrapping her arms trustingly around his neck and allowing him to lift her. He noted the spilled coffee a few feet away and the dark stains on her frilly red skirt. Without another word, he carried her to the passenger side of the SUV and belted her in. She allowed him to do it for her, moving her arms and legs like a docile child. It was terrifying, seeing this broken-down version of JJ, like whatever she'd seen had scared her so badly she didn't have the will to fight anymore.

"I want to go home," she whispered again. "My place. I don't want to be around people right now. Please."

It was the please that got him. She was so used to fighting her way through life that he knew what it cost her to ask him for anything. Despite that, he couldn't allow her to put herself in danger. Her apartment wasn't the safest place after the fire, even after all the renovations they'd done. The security there was nonexistent. Before she moved back in, Matthias was planning to wire the place up so tight even a cockroach couldn't sneak in unde-tected. And in this city, that was saying something.

"We can't do that but I know where we can go." He shut the door before she could protest or hit him with another one of those killer, big-blue gazes that made him feel like he was suffocating.

By the time he climbed into the driver's seat, JJ was quiet again, looking forlornly out the window. Her eyes were trained on the front of the Longwinds store. Had something happened while she was shopping? Had someone hurt her or scared her in one of the dressing rooms? This was New York; anything was possible.

Then she turned and their eyes met, and he shivered at the bone deep pain in her gaze. No, this wasn't just about something that happened today. JJ was running from something bigger than that.

They didn't talk as he navigated the streets, not even when he let out a curse as a group of teenagers ran right in front of the Jeep, forcing him to slam on the brakes. He pulled into an underground garage and glanced over at JJ, wondering if she'd figured out where they were going yet. Not that she'd ever seen his place. Before she'd moved in with the rest of the crew at Blake Security headquarters, they hadn't exactly been friendly enough for her to come over and hang out.

Once he got out, he came around the vehicle to open her

door. JJ looked around the dark garage nervously but she unbuckled her seatbelt. "Where are we?"

"My place." Jonas quirked an eyebrow at her surprised stare. "You said you didn't want to see anyone else. My place fits the bill."

She shrugged and then followed him to the elevator bank.

His place didn't have the advanced security they had at the Blake Security building but it was definitely a step up from most places. He swiped his card to access the elevator and then pushed the button for the tenth floor. When the elevator arrived on his floor, JJ stepped out first and then looked around curiously.

"This is a pretty nice building."

He chuckled at her surprise. "I saved my money over the years. It's not like I had much else to spend it on."

Once he opened the door, JJ gave him a small smile and elbowed past him to get inside. He let out a sigh of relief at the small show of attitude. He gave her shit about fighting with him all the time but he hadn't known how much he would miss that saucy mouth of hers. He wasn't living if he couldn't verbally banter with JJ.

"It's so clean." JJ swiped a finger over one of the tables in the living room and inspected her finger. I know this isn't your doing."

"Actually I can be a bit of a neat freak. But I have a maid service that comes once a week."

"Even though you're not here much?"

He shrugged. "Doesn't mean they should lose a client. And I'm not exactly paying rent at the penthouse."

She grinned. "That's what I said too. The no-rent situation almost makes up for my place being torched." Her smile fell then. "I thought it meant that my bad luck was over."

He opened his mouth to ask what she meant by that but the closed expression on her face changed his mind. It was more important that she feel safe right now. She'd talk when she was ready.

JJ moved from the table to the bookshelves, tilting her head slightly to examine the names on the spines. Her fingers danced over the picture frames arranged on the shelves, tapping lightly on a picture of him with his mother. Then she saw the object right next to it and her mouth fell open.

"You were a cop?"

She picked up the badge resting on the shelf and cradled it in the palm of her hand.

Jonas shivered, wishing now that he'd had time to put a few things away before he brought her here. No one ever came over, so he wasn't used to having to explain things or hide.

"I was. A long time ago."

Her eyes caught and held his. "You don't have to tell me."

There was a wealth of understanding in her voice. He could drop the subject and she'd never ask again. Something in her eyes promised that she understood not wanting to open certain boxes. She understood wanting to lock them and throw away the key forever. The idea of never opening parts of JJ made him ache. He wanted to wander around and poke through every part of her until there was no door or room in her mind that he hadn't explored. But how could he ask that of her when he wasn't willing to open himself?

"Being on the force was all I'd ever wanted. Lots of little boys want to be police officers when they grow up, but most don't know why. Maybe they like the blue uniform or Officer Friendly at their school. But I always knew why I wanted to go into law enforcement. I wanted to protect people who couldn't protect themselves. People like my mom."

JJ's eyes softened immediately. She turned to the picture on the shelf. "This is your mother? She's so beautiful."

The pain welled immediately, swelling, filling every crack and crevice until he thought he'd burst with frustration and impotent rage.

"She was beautiful. The most beautiful woman I'd ever seen."

"Was," JJ echoed sadly. "I'm so sorry."

"She died when I was in high school." He paused and took a deep breath. "She was murdered."

———

JJ couldn't help it. She gasped.

He flinched at the sound. It was such a brief reaction, and if she hadn't been looking at him she might have missed it. But before she knew what she was doing, she was across the room and in his arms. JJ squeezed him tight, resting her head in the curve of his shoulder.

She wasn't sure what she'd been expecting to hear when she started asking questions. Jonas was such a smartass most of the time that she'd just assumed he'd always gone through life with a happy-go-lucky kind of nonchalance. It was a revelation to discover that his jovial demeanor was masking some seriously painful stuff.

You aren't the only one with ghosts.

Jonas finally shifted, and she pulled back slightly so she could see his face. His forehead was pinched, like he was agitated or maybe even embarrassed.

He cleared his throat. "I'm not telling you this to ... Hell, I don't know why I'm telling you this. Maybe it's so you'll understand. The day I graduated from the police academy I felt like I'd done something for her. Something to help other women like her."

Women like me.

JJ shivered and wrapped her arms around herself to stop the shaking. If she'd been strong enough to ask for help back then, Jonas might have been one of the police officers who helped her. They could have met all those years ago.

"Your mom would be so proud of the man you've become."

His harsh laughter sounded cruel in the quiet of the room. JJ pulled back, surprised at the sound after such a serious moment.

"She wouldn't be proud of me. Instead of helping women, I just got pulled into a fucked-up situation and got kicked off the force. Not exactly how I expected things to turn out."

JJ shivered again, this time by the unexpected conflicting feelings she was experiencing. It was second nature to needle Jonas and try to get a response out of him, but this was different. This was real. The thought that he might not know how much he'd helped people, including her, was incomprehensible.

"Jonas, you saved my life."

He shook his head. "If I hadn't gotten you out of the fire, the firefighters would have. They were right behind me."

JJ shook her head again, the words she wanted so badly to say getting stuck in her throat. How could she tell him that she hadn't even been referring to the fire? It was all so messed up, and he had no idea that he was saving her life right here and now by staying with her when she felt so unstable.

"You've helped a lot of people. I know how seriously you take every single one of your cases. I normally wouldn't tell you this, but you're one of the good ones, Jonas Castillo."

His head lifted slowly, and their eyes met. This close, there was an undeniable intimacy to the position. JJ's mouth fell open as she was hit with a strong surge of desire that made her belly clench and her mouth water. Her eyes drifted closed, lulled by the sense of utter safety she felt in his arms. She nuzzled his cheek with her nose, enjoying the slight rasp of his facial hair against her skin.

Her hands lifted to rest on his shoulders, pressing against the muscles underneath the thin T-shirt he was wearing. It was no protection from her determined grip. Soon, she was kneading his shoulders while burrowing her nose deeper into the curve of his neck, trying to get farther into the safety net he created around them.

"JJ, baby, what are you doing?"

She ignored his soft whisper as her tongue snaked out to taste his skin. His neck was slightly salty and the taste was like a drug. JJ swallowed and then bit him gently on the throat. His answering groan raced through her, igniting all her nerve endings and settling like a hot ball of fire between her thighs.

Yes, this was what she needed. To be held and protected by a man who would never hurt her, only comfort and pleasure her. She hooked her arm around his neck and pulled him into a kiss. Their lips collided in a hard, passionate kiss but then Jonas pulled back.

"We shouldn't—"

"Jonas, please. I need you." She didn't wait for his answer, just moved back slightly so she could unbutton her top. His eyes followed her every movement and when she parted the material to reveal her black bra, he swallowed audibly. The strain on his face was evident.

He might not be sure about this, but he couldn't deny that he wanted her too. The knowledge gave JJ a rush of power. It was a heady thing to be able to command a man's attention like this, especially someone like Jonas who was practically a magnet for women. When she hooked her fingers in the sides of her skirt and inched it down, his fingers clenched like he had to restrain himself from reaching out and touching her.

"No, touch me," she encouraged. "I want to touch you, too."

She pressed against him, and without the fabric between them, her breasts pillowed against the hard planes of muscle. He groaned low and deep at the sensation and one hand lifted to caress one of the heavy weights. By the time they broke the kiss, they were both breathing hard and Jonas looked like he was hanging on to the reins of his control by a mere thread.

"You are so beautiful, Jessica."

His use of her first name startled her, and she was caught off guard by how much she liked hearing it on his lips. It made her feel as beautiful as he'd claimed she was, but even more than that, it made her feel like he saw her. Not just any beautiful woman but *her*. Thinking about how long they'd known each other and the things they'd been through together was overwhelming, and she tightened her arms around him.

"Please Jonas," she repeated. "I don't want to think about him. Make me forget."

His brow furrowed for a moment, but JJ didn't want to wait any longer. She jumped into his arms, and Jonas caught her. She braced her hands on his shoulders as she kissed all over his face. It took a few minutes before she realized he wasn't kissing her back. JJ stilled.

Jonas set her on her feet carefully and then knelt to get her clothes. He slipped the blouse over each of her arms and then buttoned her up with shaky fingers. Then he held out her skirt and she stepped into it on instinct.

"What is it? Why are we stopping?"

He took a deep breath. "This isn't the right time. You've just been through something that really has you spooked, and I would never take advantage of you."

Annoyed, especially because everything he said made sense, JJ pulled her skirt up roughly and turned her back to him as she righted her clothes.

When she was almost done, she felt him right behind her.

"You said 'I don't want to think about *him.*' Who were you talking about?"

JJ froze. Had she said that? She thought back frantically, all the blood draining from her face when she realized what she'd admitted aloud. "It was nothing. I was just babbling."

"*Bullshit.*" Jonas moved so he was standing right in front

of her and she couldn't avoid his eyes anymore. "Did someone try to hurt you today?"

Somehow his genuine concern was more mortifying than when he was turning her down for sex. JJ's eyes filled with tears, and she gave him her back again. He could dig into her business, follow her around, and apparently make her so hot that she forgot where she was and who she was with. But he wasn't entitled to every thought in her head or to explanations she wasn't ready to give. No one was entitled to those parts of her past. It had taken her years to learn that hard lesson.

"Take me back to the penthouse. Now."

CHAPTER NINE

Something was wrong. Something was very, very wrong with her. First of all, JJ barely tolerated him on most days. Next thing he knew, she was jumping his bones?

And you liked it.

Well, hell yeah. Because the moment her lips slid over his, every synapse in his body had lit up like a Christmas tree. He wanted her. He'd *always* wanted her.

So why don't you take advantage of that?

Because something was wrong. She wasn't acting like JJ. Yeah, under normal circumstances JJ was impetuous, loud, a little foolhardy, and said the first thing that came to her mind. But she wasn't entirely reckless. And she'd never been desperate. Not once, not ever. That kiss, her trying to climb him like a tree, that had been pure desperation. It hadn't been about him at all.

When they arrived at the penthouse, Jonas parked in the basement, in their designated spots right next to the door. And he escorted her in. The whole ride up in the elevator she said nothing to him, resolutely ignoring him with her face turned away.

Oh, so they were going to play this game. "JJ. You gotta talk to me."

"No. I don't. That's the joy of this little arrangement. I don't have to talk to you at all. Not ever."

Once the doors to the penthouse opened, she stormed out with him hot on her heels. Matthias came out of the kitchen holding a tub of rocky road. "Hey, Jonas, I was thinking that we could –"

JJ interrupted his flow of conversation by bumping his shoulder as she stormed by him.

She mumbled a brief apology but kept right on marching to her bedroom. Matthias brought his attention to Jonas. "What happened?"

"I have no fucking idea. But I'm sure as hell going to find out."

Jonas followed her, but he heard Matthias whisper behind them, "Maybe that's not the best idea you've ever had?"

Jonas ignored him. What the hell did he know?

What the hell do you know is a better question.

What he knew was that JJ tasted fucking incredible. That's what he knew. He also knew that something was eating at her. Burrowing deep inside her, and she was gonna blow. What he didn't know was why it was so important to him that she not self-destruct. That whatever was bothering her was better out than in. And he wanted to help her.

Why, because you're Captain freaking America? No. Because despite their constant fighting, he cared about her. She was smart, funny, and fuck, she was sexy. And he wanted her.

Yeah, but that want had been eating at him for years now. This wasn't about that. He was worried. Something was wrong. He didn't bother to knock; he just barged into her bedroom.

"Knock much?" She whirled on him, her movements quick and angry as she rolled her shoulders.

"Well, I knew you wouldn't say come in, and something is clearly up with you." He closed the door and locked it.

Her gaze widened and pinned to the lock. *What the hell?*

That wasn't the anger he was used to seeing, that was cold fear. Jonas frowned and unlocked the door, and then stepped away from it about three feet, giving her clear access if she wanted to get out. "See, I'm not trying to keep you in here. I just want to talk to you. Something is going on. You haven't been acting like yourself for weeks. And now you're mad at me because I wasn't an asshole?"

"Yes you were."

Jonas crossed arms. "Explain to me *how* I was an asshole. A woman who most of the time is screaming at me, or calling me names, or trying to throw things at me, suddenly decides that she wants to jump my bones. Wraps herself around me, tasting like sugar and sin and everything I could want. But she's not acting like herself. So, instead of backing her up against the wall and sinking inside her so deep that neither one of us can remember our names, I back off because I want to know what's wrong with her. Oh, and I also want her to want me for *me.* Not because she's pissed off or upset, or scared. And somehow that makes me an asshole?"

JJ blinked at him. "Wow, that's the most words I've heard you use in a row ever."

"I talk plenty."

"Not to me you don't."

"Yeah well. You don't talk to me much either. You shout."

"That's because you needle me."

Jonah shook his head. "I'm not here to fight." He held up his hands. "What I am here to do is try and find out what's going on. Because you haven't been acting like yourself and I am fucking worried. So out with it."

When her eyes welled with tears, Jonas's blood froze in his veins. *Fuck.* He hated tears. "I want you to be okay. Yeah, we needle each other. But I do care about what happens to you. And you're sexy. But then again, you know that already. But more than I want you, more than I want sex, I want you to be okay. And you're clearly not."

She swiped a tear with the back of her hand. "You really are a good guy, aren't you?"

Her voice was soft; there was no edge to it. No edge to

her. Her shoulders slumped forward and he saw that she was defeated. What the hell did she mean by that?

"I am. Mostly. Sometimes. Fuck, not always. But if you need help, or are in trouble, or something is wrong, then I'm your guy." He just prayed to God she told him. Because he didn't have the strength to turn her down again if she wound her body around his.

————

JJ wasn't even sure what made her start talking to him. Maybe it was something in his eyes. Maybe it was the gentleness of his tone. But either way, all she wanted to do was curl up into a ball and get a really good hug. Jonas moved forward slowly then took her hand. "Gotta talk to someone sometime, JJ. How about me?"

She nodded and then eased down onto her bed and waited for Jonas to sit next to her. This was not exactly the kind of action she'd planned with him. *Did you really plan that at all? Or were you operating on fear?*

Okay, she wasn't going to examine that right now. She was too raw. There was too much going on inside. "I've had really bad luck with guys. The worst kind."

"I wouldn't say you have bad luck. You maybe just haven't found the right one."

She shook her head. "When I say bad luck, I don't mean that a guy insisted that I pay for everything, even though I have had one of those, or that he lived with his parents, although I've had one of those too. I've had the kind of people that shouldn't be with anyone, the kind of guys that make me feel bad about myself. Those kind of guys—"

His voice was low and hushed when he spoke. There was also a hint of an edge to it. As if he was starting to see what she was talking about. "You deserve so much more."

She nodded. "I'm sorry. I'm blabbering on. It's just this project at work is making me feel like I'm back in that place again. Where I've been hurt by someone so deeply but have no one to talk to."

He was silent for a long moment then asked softly, "What about Lucia?"

She sniffed away the tears. "Lucia is the best friend a girl could ever ask for. But when her brother died, she was broken. Really, *really* broken for a really long time. It was that kind of visceral pain and loss. Even now, knowing that everything worked out for her, I can still see the look of pain in her eyes at the funeral. I can *still* feel her grief. And I wasn't going to burden her with my shit. None of that would be fair. So while she was hurting in her own way, I was hurting in another. I never told her because, you know Lucia. She would feel guilty. And there was nothing for her to feel guilty about. She'd lost her brother. She was entitled to crumble."

"I don't know. I know that if you sat down and talked to her now she'd probably understand why you didn't tell her, and wish that she could have been there for you. Maybe it would help to talk to her now?"

JJ shook her head. "No. Her life is finally the way that it should be. Rafe is back. She has Noah and that beautiful baby." Last year had been one hell of a roller coaster ride. Even if she'd been inclined to share all her deep dark and scaries with her bestie, they'd all had a few things to deal with.

Things like someone trying to kill Lucia. Lucia discovering her brother had been alive all that time. Somehow JJ's past problems hadn't made the top of the list.

"She's your friend. She would want to help."

"I'm not bringing her into any of this." Lucia didn't deserve that.

"You're still not going to tell me what's going on?" Jonas asked.

She shook her head. "Enough. It's just been a long day. I freaked out over ... It's okay. I think I just need someone to distract me right now. Do you think you can do that?"

CHAPTER TEN

S hit, he wanted her. Jonas had never felt more pressure to make a kiss perfect. But this was JJ and she needed him. It was about so much more than desire.

Looking down at her face, he took in the details that had teased him for so long. The blond hair that always seemed tousled and messy. The blue eyes that should have looked innocent but always had a twinkle of mischief. The peaches-and-cream skin that taunted him to take a bite. She was so beautiful.

"What are you waiting for?" JJ teased. "Do it already."

He groaned. His dick responded to the words *do it* as if she'd been speaking straight to him directly.

"Always busting my balls, aren't you?"

She grinned. "That's what I live for."

"Maybe I need to give that smart mouth something else to do."

Before she could respond to that, Jonas pulled her up slightly so he could fit his lips over hers. It was so perfect, the way they notched together like puzzle pieces. It was a little scary how well they fit, like they'd been made for each other but were just getting around to discovering that. It probably wasn't the smartest thing, starting something with JJ while she was obviously confused and a little scared about what was happening. She needed to feel safe and secure, and Jonas would never want to pressure her into anything. The mature thing to do would be to end this, whatever it was, then ask her out for a drink after it was resolved.

He pulled back and looked down at the wide blue eyes watching him like he was a savior and a sinner all in one. She made a little whimper in the back of her throat, a hoarse, needy sound that instantly threw Jonas from foreplay into full-scale need. What was it about this woman that made him lose all control? Around JJ he was nothing but instinct and sensation, his years of experience and finesse going right out the window.

"You really have me all twisted up, you know?"

The statement wasn't exactly a compliment, but JJ beamed. He should have known his little troublemaker would love the idea of throwing him off his game. Not that it mattered. Whatever she wanted he was happy to give. Just the thought of JJ needing something and not coming to him for it gave him a deep sense of dissatisfaction. It would have sounded ridiculous just a few months ago, but he was starting to understand exactly why Noah looked happier than ever but also way more stressed. Worrying about someone else constantly took its toll.

Despite how badly he wanted to strip her naked and do all the things he'd dreamed of doing to that luscious body, Jonas felt obligated to at least try to be the voice of reason.

"Are you sure about this, baby? We don't have to do anything. I can just hold you if you want."

JJ scowled. "Jesus, what does a girl have to do to get a little satisfaction?" She squealed when he suddenly leaped on her, burying his face in her neck.

"That's it. Now you're in for it," he growled against her

skin, noting how she shivered as the words brushed over her skin.

Experimentally, he trailed the tip of his tongue up the soft skin of her neck until he reached her ear. She sighed when he took the lobe between his teeth gently.

"That feels so good," she purred. Her hands moved over his shoulders gently, clutching at them when his tongue dipped into the shell of her ear. "I've dreamed about this so many times."

Surprised, Jonas lifted his head. "You dreamed about me?"

She bit her lip, looking slightly bashful. "I used to fight with you and then sneak in here and imagine that you followed me. That you wanted me the same way I wanted you. Like it was so intense you could barely breathe."

His eyes gleamed. "That's exactly how I want you, JJ. You make me lose my head completely. With you, I feel like I have no control."

One of her hands lifted, tentatively to his face. "So let go then. Just do whatever you feel."

Jonas groaned. That kind of freedom was dangerous. There were so many things he wanted to do and feel with her that he didn't know where to start. Then her fingers brushed over his lips and instinctively he opened, nipping at her fingers gently. Her sudden intake of breath sent a stab of desire bolting down his spine. It was suddenly, desperately urgent that he taste her again. Everywhere.

He leaned down and covered her mouth with his. JJ was right there with him, a willing participant, sucking and licking and biting. God, those sounds she made and the way her fingers clenched in his hair. He couldn't get enough of her.

Hands tugged at her clothing and then his own, frantic to get skin to skin. The next few moments were a blur as they tussled to get free without breaking the kiss. Jonas didn't want to separate from her for even a minute. Maybe a part of him was afraid that if he let this moment go, it would disappear.

JJ didn't seem to have any hesitation about undressing, either. The sight of the lacy white panties she wore only cranked his desire higher. Not wasting any time, Jonas yanked her closer and buried his face between her legs. Her soft cries egged him on as he tasted her. He didn't even bother to take the panties off, just pulled them to the side. Something about not waiting made it even hotter.

JJ purred and cried with every lash of his tongue. Jonas felt like a man possessed as he licked and sucked until she screamed her release. Panting, JJ didn't even get a chance to catch her breath before he was on her, nuzzling between her soft breasts. Her arms wrapped around him languidly with a satisfied laziness that made him very happy.

"Damn," she said finally. That one word carried a world of meaning.

"Yeah. The best you've ever had, huh?" As he'd hoped, the cocky words made her smile.

"Actually it was. You're amazing."

It was so unexpected to hear her compliment him when he'd been expecting the usual snarky reply. Pleasure curled through Jonas and made him feel like he was lit from within.

"It is for me, too. Everything with you is amazing. I hope you know that, Jessica Jones."

The sudden flush on her cheeks told him that he'd pleased her, and the thought made him happy, too. What the hell was happening to him? He'd never cared this much about a woman's approval before. Before he had time to examine it too closely, JJ arched her back, pressing her body against his, wiping all rational thought from his brain.

Then she reached into his boxers and wrapped delicate fingers around his hard cock. Jonas bit the inside of his cheek to keep from blowing his load like a teenager.

"It seems I'm the only one who's had my fun," JJ teased. "You've been keeping this from me."

"Not anymore," Jonas groaned. He reached for his wallet for a condom and had it on in record time. Under different circumstances he'd have spent more time getting her ready, but if JJ felt what he did, any more ready would cause a heart attack.

He settled between her legs and they both cried out at the pressure. Jonas rocked against her, sliding through her slick heat. JJ whimpered and her nails dug into his back.

"You ready, baby?" He swiveled his hips again.

"Hurry up or I'll kill you!"

He chuckled, but the laugh died in his throat when she canted her hips forward and he slipped inside. Jonas wasn't ready for the intense pressure and sense of rightness being enveloped in her heat. Then JJ wrapped her arms around his shoulders and pulled him down for another kiss, and the sense of rightness just magnified. This was where he was meant to be and who he was meant to be with.

"Oh my God, so good," JJ cried, her eyes on his, wide and trusting.

Her pussy clamped down, and they groaned together. For a moment, he was suspended in time, and Jonas wondered if he'd actually died and gone to heaven. If this was how he went, clutched in the tightest, hottest pussy he'd ever encountered, he figured it was a risk worth taking.

"Fuck, you're so tight."

JJ mewled and wrapped her long legs around his waist, holding him against her. It was like being enclosed in heat, the action spurring him to take her harder. Soon he was lost in the sound of her cries and the firm grasp of her muscles squeezing his cock as she came continuously.

JJ was in trouble. So much trouble.

After what felt like having ten orgasms in a row, she could barely catch her breath. But Jonas was still hard. The man had just fucked her to within an inch of losing consciousness and he wasn't done yet.

So much fucking trouble.

He swiveled his hips, as if to remind her that he was still there. Like she could forget. JJ snorted softly at her own joke.

"Am I amusing you, Miss Jones?" There was an erotic threat in the soft timbre of his voice that made her shiver.

She peeked up at him through lowered lashes. JJ was used to being snarky and argumentative with Jonas. It was Jonas after all, her favorite target when she was feeling bitchy. But now she would never be able to look at him the same way again. The man was a marathoner in the bedroom and hung like a stallion. How the hell could she argue with him knowing what he was packing beneath his clothes now?

"I wasn't laughing at you. Definitely not," JJ finally muttered.

His eyes heated and he thrust again, making her gasp softly. "Good, because I'm not done with you yet. You ready for more?"

She was going to be sore, but she didn't care. "Yes, please."

It was his turn to chuckle, but he didn't make her wait. He pulled her down by hooking his arms under her knees. Once she was in a better position, he brushed his thumb over her clit. JJ's mouth fell open as she tried to gain control of her breathing. She'd just come and was already on the edge again.

"Look at me," Jonas rasped. His deep voice would forever be a part of her erotic dreams.

When she finally met his eyes, he let loose a deep growl that instantly made her wetter. Suddenly it was all too much. This was Jonas, her friend and sometimes enemy, and she was right on the brink of losing herself in him. Trusting a man with everything hadn't worked out so well in the past.

As if he could sense her fear, Jonas cupped her cheeks.

"I've got you, sweetheart. It's okay. I just want to make you feel good."

The simple words meant so much more than he could ever know.

"You do. You feel so good."

JJ clutched at his arms, overwhelmed at not only the physical sensations of taking him deep inside, but the sense of closeness. She'd never felt this close to anyone, not even the one man who'd taught her never to trust again. But she couldn't think about that now, not when she'd come so far and felt safe for the first time in a long time. That was how Jonas made her feel. Safe and protected and … loved.

Jonas's fingers tightened under her shoulders, holding her captive as he slid deeper. His harsh breaths in her ear increased, and to JJ it was the most erotic sound in the world. This was all so new to her, and she was a little scared to examine it too closely, but there was no denying their physical connection. She'd never had this reaction to a man before, like she could completely let go and be safe and secure in his arms with no judgment. Only Jonas had ever made her feel this free. She loved it and reveled in the erotic power she held over him.

Experimentally, she tightened her muscles around him. His groan was the sexiest thing she'd ever heard.

"Fuck! Your pussy just clamped down on me."

JJ looked him in the eye, holding his gaze as she deliberately tightened her muscles again. His jaw clenched and he closed his eyes in an expression that was a cross between agony and ecstasy.

"You are fucking perfect, you know that?"

His low sexy growl in her ear sent her flying and everything splintered into fragments of light and color.

CHAPTER ELEVEN

Matthias could see the bloody writing on the wall. The way Jonas and JJ were going, things were hitting a fucking tipping point. And the way Jonas had gone in that room after her, followed by silence and then, well yeah, Matthias had had to put on his noise canceling headphones once the moaning started.

Granted, the two of them had been circling each other for God knew how long now. It was bound to happen. He just prayed that they wouldn't be nearly as disgusting as Noah and Lucia. Those two could barely keep their hands off each other. Even when she was pregnant.

You thought she looked gorgeous pregnant. All glowy skin and tits to—

He shoved the thought aside. For the most part, he managed to keep the wayward Lucia thoughts to himself ...deep down, hidden in the dark. But sometimes he couldn't help it. They had a much more appropriate relationship now. Not that they'd had any kind of *inappropriate* relationship.

Oh bollocks. He had much more appropriate feelings about her now. But every now and again, he would wish for someone like her for himself.

As if that was ever going to happen. *What normal girl was going to want a twenty-five year old virgin with a pierced dick?* Yeah. There was that.

No, he'd just stick to his computers for now and try and ignore the people coupling off around him. At the very least, he had the rest of the guys.

An alarm chimed, alerting him that someone was accessing his restricted files. He frowned and immediately opened up the server access window. He kept the personnel files in a separate server, hidden under lock and key, under a mountain of shit. They were completely encrypted, and even if someone was able to decrypt the files, everything was in code. So what the hell? Who was in here?

He peeled off one of the headphones only to hear a distant moan again. Damn it. The two of them were going to become a problem. But he had bigger fish to fry right now. He pulled out his phone and quickly tapped out a message to Noah.

This was too urgent to fuck with their usual clandestine methodology. In seconds his phone was ringing.

"What's the problem?"

Noah was at Lucia's grandmother's house. They'd taken Isabella over there for a family dinner. Usually Nonna came to the penthouse and cooked for everyone, but the family needed some alone time.

"Someone just tried to access personnel files."

There was a beat of silence. "What do you mean *someone?*"

"Not sure exactly. Access codes were attempted. But I've closed off whatever opening they tried to use. I didn't know if it was deliberate though. I was hoping it was you trying to get in and that you just forgot to let me know first."

"Fuck."

"I might be wrong." It was unlikely that he was. "Might've been a system error or something. But I don't like to fuck around with that kind of stuff. So figured I'd call and check. You're the only other one who has access."

"Not me. Lock it down if it's a system glitch. But what is your gut telling you?"

His gut told him all hell was about to break loose. But he wasn't telling Noah that right now. The guy was with his wife, trying to have some much needed family time. "Gut tells me trouble. But I've got an eye on it; the data is locked down and nearly impossible to read. If it is someone trying to break in, they'll have to try again. And I'll be waiting."

"With a machete and a hacksaw?"

Matthias smirked. "Too bloody right." In his field days, when he'd been an agent for ORUS, his weapons of choice had been knives. Knives were personal. Knives conveyed a message.

But you're not that person anymore.

No, no he wasn't. Now he didn't kill people because someone told him to. And that was a balm to his soul. But if he did have trouble, he would fight like the devil to protect his newfound soul. And to protect his family. The family he'd made for himself.

Next time someone came knocking, they were going to get a nasty surprise.

———

The next night, JJ pushed aside the heavy glass door and stepped out into the balmy spring evening. She knew the rules. Get directly into a cab and go straight home. She'd gotten an earful from Noah after the last time. And Matthias. Even Oskar had found a way to tell her that she needed to be more careful. She was just about to hop into a cab when she saw the black SUV parked at the curb and recognized the driver.

Unable to help the smile, she slowly strolled over to Jonas, making sure to emphasize the sway in her hips. When he rolled the window down and leaned over, her heart caught just a little. *You should not be feeling this way. You are going to get hurt by feeling this way. This is dangerous. Don't you understand that?*

She did understand. But the knowledge didn't stop her

from feeling. When he leaned over, his smile was rakish. "You should get in the car with me."

"My mother warned me about guys like you. You're going to drag me off somewhere and do all sorts of debauched things to me."

He raised a brow. "Is that an invitation?"

She shook her head and giggled. "Possibly."

"Get in. We're going to go eat."

"I love how you just dictate these things."

Jonas shrugged and said, "So you're not hungry for a home-cooked, classic Spanish meal?" Her stomach rumbled. And he chuckled low. "Your stomach knows what's up. Get in."

Like she was really going to say no to a home-cooked meal. From what she'd heard, he was an amazing cook. She would eat pretty much anything the man put in front of her right now. She was starving.

"You know, you didn't have to come pick me up. I was going to behave and take a cab."

"I know. I wanted to."

As she climbed into the car, his slow perusal of her body told her everything she needed to know. He was thinking about the other night. Of them in bed. Of the way he'd made her scream with just a few simple touches. The way he'd made her heart race. He was thinking about every touch, every movement, every breath. She knew that because that's exactly what she was thinking about. Just being next to him, her skin hummed with anticipation and awareness.

She cleared her throat. "So, Mr. Castillo, tell me, where did you learn to cook?"

"Well, my mom only had me. So there was really no one else to pass her secrets on to."

"So you became the daughter she never had?"

Jonas grumbled that sexy, low laugh, just as she'd hoped he would. "Something like that. I'm glad she taught me. Now I use the skill to impress beautiful women."

JJ shook her head and grinned even though she tried not to. "Seriously. I do appreciate the ride."

"You're welcome. But you know it's nothing. If you call any one of us, we'll come get you."

When they passed the boutique where she'd gotten the

blast from the past, she couldn't help the small shiver that came over her. "I know. And I should use it more. I just, I get caught up in being independent, you know? I had a spook the other day. It reminded me that with everything we've had going on in the last year or so, maybe I should take advantage of the big burly security team I have at my disposal. One guy in particular."

Jonas gave her a knowing smile. When they reached his apartment, she noticed a couple of little changes and additions. He'd added a purse hook right next to the door. That hadn't been there the last time she'd been here. And when he turned on the lights, they immediately went dim and were far more subdued than she remembered. Music started to play faintly, a low and sexy sound that sounded like Trip Hop or something. "Mr. Castillo, something tells me that you planned all of this."

He shrugged out of his jacket and then hung his holster next to it. "Who, me?"

"Yes, you. This looks like mood lighting."

"That's because it *is* mood lighting," he said with a laugh before leading her into the kitchen. "Here, you chop the onions."

"Oh man, how come I get the dirty job?"

He chuckled low and throaty, a familiar sound to her now. He made that sound when he was happy, truly happy and relaxed. *Yeah, like when he's inside you.*

"No one eats for free. All the jobs are dirty if they're done right. And that's the way we like it," he said with a wink.

For the next hour, they worked side by side. Chopping, cutting, stirring. He made her laugh. He danced with her a little and regaled her with the happier memories of his mother.

She told him about the places she wanted to visit, the things she wanted to see. Her last trip to Europe as well. It turned out they knew a lot of the same people in the fashion industry. How he knew people in the fashion industry confused her though.

"Let me guess, you dated a model or two?"

He grinned. "A gentleman never tells."

"Come on. If you have dated a bona fide model, I'll be disgusted, and then I will also be insanely jealous."

"How would you feel knowing that I'd walked a runway or two myself when I was on holiday visiting my grandmother?"

Oh, she believed him all right. He had the looks, the body. Lord help her, the face. And he was just crazy enough to do something like that on a whim. This also explained his ridiculous love of clothing.

"Of course you were a model."

He rolled his eyes. "Like you couldn't be yourself."

JJ snorted. "Come on. I'm just Jessica Jones from Queens. Not a model."

"But you easily could've been. You're not super tall, but the face ... and I will attest to the magnificent body."

A flush crept up her neck, and she ducked her head as she stirred the sauce. "Jonas Castillo, flattery will get you everywhere."

"Right now, I'll settle for flattery getting me a kiss."

He wrapped an arm around her waist and slid his hand along her arm, gently caressing until they were stirring the pot of sauce together. And then he kissed her neck.

For a moment, JJ couldn't believe that this was her life. It was all so wonderfully *normal*. Like Jonas Castillo was just this hot guy that she was interested in. And they were just standing here stirring sauce like any other normal couple would do.

You can't have this. Because even though this is great for now, your past will ruin it.

She couldn't let herself get too close. Because if she did, she was going to get her heart ripped out.

CHAPTER TWELVE

It took about an hour to finish cooking and JJ had never had so much fun making a meal. It was strange because she'd never been much of a cook, but being with Jonas made everything fun. For the next hour she decided to put away all her worries and just live in the moment. After all, what was life if she couldn't enjoy a good meal with a handsome man?

"This looks delicious," she said.

They worked together bringing dishes over to the small dining room table. JJ looked around curiously. It was a nice apartment, altogether too fancy for a single man living alone. She remembered the tarnished police badge on the bookshelf. There was so much she didn't know about him. Was it so hard to believe that perhaps he'd had a family in another life? Maybe he hadn't always lived here alone.

Jonas shrugged. "My mom taught me to enjoy good food. So I try to keep up my skills. She's looking down on me. Got to make her proud."

There was something about the way he said it that made JJ pause. After the day he'd confided about his mother's murder, she'd tried hard not to pry. She enjoyed giving Jonas a hard time because he was pompous, annoying, and way too sexy. But she never would have guessed he had so much going on underneath the surface. The badass exterior was deceptive. He was really a sweet guy.

"Why would you think she isn't proud?" JJ asked. From everything that she'd seen, Jonas was a perfect son, the kind that any mother would be proud of.

"I'm sure she is," he replied. But he wouldn't meet her eyes. "Can you grab the wine?"

Jonas kept his eyes down as he set the table. Okay then. That was a clear sign he didn't want to talk about it. *Noted.*

JJ went back to the kitchen to grab the bottle of wine they'd started working on earlier. By the time she got back, Jonas was already dishing the tapas they'd made onto plates. The fragrant scent of seasoned chicken, vegetables, and cheese filled the air.

JJ stomach growled. "I can't wait to dig in."

And just like that Jonas's smile was back. "That's what I love to see. A woman with an appetite."

"Well if that's what you like, get ready for a treat. I don't miss meals." JJ picked up a plate with a big smile. "I'm sure my ass tells the true story."

"Your ass torments me, that's what it does," Jonas muttered.

JJ paused in the act of loading the soft corn tortilla on her plate with meat. She bit her lip and glanced over at Jonas. He held her gaze, not backing down. *Oh Jesus.* Blood rushed to her face and she hurriedly threw toppings on her plate, not even looking at what she was getting.

"That's right, eat up. You'll need your energy later." Jonas grinned as she added another tapas on top of the two she already had. If the man was going to make erotic promises like that, she wasn't going to discourage him.

For a moment, all was quiet as they enjoyed their food, but it was a comfortable silence. JJ tried not to stare at him but it was hard. He was handsome, yes, but more than that, he was kind. She'd never thought she could have this sort of easy, comfortable routine with a man, where she was completely fine just hanging out doing nothing. For so long, she'd thought of men as always having an agenda. The thought of trusting any man had been incomprehensible. No man would have ever been able to get that close anyway.

But somehow Jonas had snuck past every single one of her defenses and become an essential part of her everyday life. With her living at the penthouse and him over so often, he'd quickly become an integral part of her life.

She couldn't imagine waking up in the morning without seeing him in his workout clothes, sweaty from a long run in the penthouse gym. And now it was even harder to imagine her evenings without him. Who would she talk to or rant to about the crazy stuff that happened at work? Who could she call that would drop everything just because she felt uneasy and needed to hear a familiar voice?

Lucia would drop everything for you. You know she would.

JJ felt an unmistakable rush of sadness at the thought. Because even though it was true, Lucia had a family now that had to take precedence over anything else. Including her friendship. And that was the way it should be. The circle of life. The bubbly girl she'd grown up with was now a wife and a mother.

JJ had no part of that. Lucia had created a new family and JJ was only on the outskirts looking in.

I'm jealous, she realized. Not in a bad way, she was thrilled that her best friend had found the love she deserved. But there was no denying that she missed her place in Lucia's life and longed to find that kind of love for herself.

"You're quiet. Whenever you're quiet it's either because something bad happened that you don't want me to find out about or because you're plotting something you don't want me to find out about."

JJ smiled at his attempt to cheer her up. "Neither this time. I was just thinking about work."

He narrowed his eyes at the obvious lie. "What's going on at work? Has anything else strange happened?"

Now she felt bad. She'd just been trying to throw him off the scent of her melancholy feelings about her best friend, not worry him.

"Nothing like that. It's actually about this charity event I'm working on. It's to benefit victims of domestic violence. Working with them has been intense. Brings up a lot of old memories."

That actually wasn't a lie, JJ conceded. It had been intense working with Alison, planning the makeup seminars that they'd finally decided to do once a week. JJ pushed the last bits of chicken around her plate with her fork. When she thought back to how reluctant she'd been to get involved in the beginning, she was ashamed. It had brought up some bad memories, of course, but it had also been cathartic in a way. When Alison described some of the women she was currently working with, JJ recognized herself in their stories. She understood their fear, their hesitation to take a chance and trust someone to help them.

It was incredibly daunting but also humbling. Maybe they weren't the only ones in need of healing.

"Old memories?" Jonas's mouth flattened into a thin line and JJ knew the moment he got it. "Someone hurt you."

JJ swallowed, her throat suddenly dry as dust. "It was a long time ago. It doesn't matter now."

"It matters," Jonas rasped, his jaw working furiously. "Everything about you matters to me."

It was such a simple statement, but it meant the world to JJ. She closed her eyes and willed the damnable tears back. Her emotions had been dangerously close to the surface lately, but that was a line she couldn't cross. She'd already screwed up and cried in front of him once before.

"I was really young. Really insecure. And he made me feel special. Even when things escalated, when he hit me or threatened to kill me, he always made it seem like he did those things because he was so desperate to keep me. Because I drove him to it. It was overwhelming for a teenage girl."

His hand covered his mouth. "You were that young?"

JJ shrugged. "It was right after Rafe died. Lucia was a mess and I was, too. I'd never known anyone who died before. I had no idea how to process it. Then I met D— then I met a guy."

He didn't say anything for a long time, and suddenly JJ was slammed with a sense of foreboding. Why had she told him any of that? It never went well when guys found out about her past. They either went into hero mode and felt like they needed to save her from her damaged past or they were overwhelmed and got distant. The thought of Jonas distancing himself from her hurt.

"Never mind. I don't know why I'm telling you all of this."

He reached across the table and took her hand gently in his. She was so shocked that she jolted before her eyes flew up to meet his. JJ relaxed slightly when she saw no judgment in his eyes.

"I want you to tell me anything you want to. I want to know you, Jessica Jones. Inside and out."

———

Jonas scooted his chair over to her side of the table so he was mere inches away from her. He didn't move at all, as if afraid to distract her from talking.

"I'm sure it seems stupid to you that I didn't just kick him to the curb."

"No, it doesn't seem stupid at all."

Her head tilted slightly at his statement. Suddenly, Jonas

pulled her closer. She went still as a board at first but then slowly relaxed, resting her head on his chest with a sigh.

"When I was a little boy, I didn't understand that my family was different."

JJ looked up, her attention drawn by the soft, vulnerable tone of his voice. She didn't dare interrupt, though. Even though he'd told her that his mother had been murdered the first time he'd taken her to his apartment, he'd never mentioned it again. It wasn't the kind of thing she'd ever ask about, either. Jonas was such a closed book sometimes, but she'd always sensed there was a reason he was so closed off.

"My father was well liked in our neighborhood. He was good with cars, and anything with an engine actually, so he was always helping everyone out with repairs. Everyone thought he was a great guy."

He was quiet for so long that JJ thought he wasn't going to continue. Tears stung her eyes.

His mother was murdered. Oh God.

"He wasn't a great guy, was he?" she murmured. "Not to you and your mother."

"No, he wasn't. It was a hard lesson to learn so young.

That people can be so charming in public and then be a monster behind closed doors. But I learned."

Her arms tightened around his waist. "I'm so sorry, Jonas. And here I am telling you about my situation when you've lived through so much worse."

"I'm glad you told me. Pain isn't a competition. I just wanted you to know that I'm not going to ever judge you for the decisions you've made. Because I understand how hard it is to walk away from someone you care about, even when they're hurting you."

"That's just it. I wasn't strong enough to walk away. He left me. Just vanished. I still don't know exactly why. Maybe I have a guardian angel out there or something."

Jonas pulled her forward and kissed her hair. "Thank God for that. My mother never had that. If she had, maybe things would have been different. I wonder about that every day."

"She would be so proud of you. You help people all the time. All those women who come to Blake Security for protection, you make them feel safe."

Jonas shook his head sadly. "The one thing I couldn't do for her."

She had no idea what to say to that, so she pulled him close for a hug. After a moment of hesitation, Jonas grabbed her and buried his face in her neck. They stayed like that for a long time, until Jonas suddenly coughed and wiped under his eyes discreetly.

JJ took a sip of wine to give him a moment of privacy. Finally, he let out a deep sigh.

"Thank you. I needed to say that. I haven't talked about her in so long. For years it was just too difficult, and then I thought that it was better to just focus on the future instead of the past. But I don't want to forget her. I won't let him take that from me, too."

JJ could understand that. Even though she wasn't as close to her family as she'd like, she couldn't imagine life without her mother to hover over her or her dad's gruff encouragement. They were very different people and hadn't understood her flighty, artistic ways, but they'd loved her the best they could.

"Tell me about your mother. What was she like?"

Jonas smiled and the sight of it took her off guard. He looked so young and carefree when he smiled. JJ was filled with a deep longing to see that look on his face every day.

"She liked to cook. And to embroider pillows. She was always making something. They didn't always come out the way she wanted, but she didn't care. I think she just enjoyed the process of creating something beautiful from nothing."

"That's how I feel about fashion," JJ commented. "My parents never really understood where my love for it came from. But I love the idea that you can find beauty all around. Color can make people happy so easily. But I think my parents wished I was more practical. You know, responsible."

"You are responsible," Jonas said.

"I am. But I meant in a more general sense. My parents wanted a child more like you. Someone using their life to be an advocate for people in need. Doing things to make the world a better place."

JJ shook her head bashfully at Jonas's intense look. She definitely didn't want to rehash all the ways she'd been a disappointment to her parents.

CHAPTER THIRTEEN

Jonas studied JJ. "Do you have any idea how strong you are? I know you don't feel it, but I see that strength in you every day."

"Sometimes I just need a reminder that I'm not that girl anymore."

He pulled her closer and lifted the wine glass out of her hands. "Let me take that. And I'll remind you that you are sexy, sassy, and can bring a man to his knees."

"Wait, I'm not finished ye—"

"Don't worry. You can sip it off of me later."

Her lips formed an O. He tugged her into the bedroom,

closing the door behind them. "You all right with this? We can stop at any time if you're not."

"Y-yeah." She licked her lips.

Jonas set the wine glass on the bedside table. When he turned to pull her toward him, his hands shook a little. What the hell was wrong with him? He'd already been with her once. Were his hands freaking shaking? Like he was a rookie or something? *Because this time you know what's going to happen. You know how explosive this can be.*

Stepping in front of her, Jonas let his hands span her waist, bringing her flush against him. She gasped, and her eyes snapped to his. The thundering of his heartbeat was all he could hear as he focused on her parted lips.

He dipped his head, kissing her softly. Immediately, she sighed into his mouth and wound her hands into the hair at the nape of his neck. She sucked his tongue into her hot, wet mouth, and Jonas forgot for a moment that he was supposed to be taking things slow. Focusing on drawing this out. He only wanted to keep tasting her.

While she tried to wrestle control of the kiss from him, his hands fisted in the material of her skirt, and he tugged it up. Her sudden shocked intake of breath was all he needed to take control again, and he lifted her up until she wrapped her legs around him, but he didn't deposit her on the bed. Instead, he turned them to the door and braced her against it. "Just relax. I'm going to take care of you, JJ."

She used his shoulders as leverage and arched her body so that her slick heat met the bulge in his slacks. She worked her hips in a figure eight, and Jonas's eyes crossed. She knew how to move her body. Knew how to work him over.

"JJ." Her name was more grunt than English, but lust chased desire along his nerve endings, and the part of his brain that focused on the finer points of language had long overheated.

He had to find a way to gain control again.

He reluctantly removed her hands from the nape of his neck and lifted them above her head as he encircled them. He licked at her lips, and very deliberately, he slid his cock against the satin undies that blocked his path to bliss.

She hissed. "Jonas. Hurry please."

No. He was not rushing this. Tonight he wanted to take his time. "Look at me, JJ."

Her lids fluttered open, and her pupils were dilated. As

he kissed her again, his body rocked against hers, and she met every movement of his hips with her own. "You want me to take you like this? Hard and fast and up against the wall?" Fuck the idea made his skin burn.

"At this point I could give two shits how you take me just as long as you're inside me. I'm not going to be picky."

"Hmm." He nuzzled her neck as he slipped his hand under her blouse. When his palm closed over the full globe, they both moaned. Her breasts were so full and firm. So soft and responsive.

"Jonas, please."

He kissed her again deeply, savoring the flavor of the wine on her tongue and sucking on it until she moaned and her body started to rock into his in a steady rhythm.

Slowly, he backed away from the kiss. Releasing her hands, he steadied her by the waist and set her feet back on the floor. Her eyes went wide with questions, but she didn't say anything. She merely followed his silent command, and he turned her around. Skimming his hands over the flesh of her arms, he positioned her palms against the door. He took his time, caressing her. When his hands reached the buttons on her blouse, she stiffened.

Slowly, he popped each button from its tiny loop. With each one he released, she puffed out a small breath, then finally exhaled completely when he had her blouse fully open. He peeled the fine silk off her shoulder, kissed the soft skin of her back as the material fell away. Her skin was satin smooth; he could do nothing but touch it and never get bored.

"Jonas, what are you doing?"

"I'm taking care of you."

When he unhooked her bra, she groaned. He didn't let her bring down her hands so he couldn't remove it. Instead, he skimmed his hands up her torso, palming her softly, then gently massaging. Her legs started to quiver when the massage turned from relief to sensual tease. Gently, he plucked the pebbled tips, and she dropped her forehead against the wall.

"You'll have to forgive me, but I've had a mild obsession with your breasts since I first saw you. I have no doubt spent countless hours thinking about how they would taste, what the weight of them would be like in my palms, how sensitive they were, if you would mind me using my teeth."

Her breath came out ragged and sharp. "Jonas. I can't. You're killing me."

He plucked the tight buds again. "If you want me to stop, all you have to do is say so."

He continued to trail hot, open-mouthed kisses across her shoulders and the back of her neck as he played.

When she started to rotate her hips back against him, he swore and gritted his teeth at the red haze of lust clouding his vision. Dropping his hands to her hips, he stopped them. "Just relax, sweetheart." He'd always known it would be like this between them. A fight for control. And he didn't mind it. But tonight, he wanted her to know that she could trust him. That if she gave just a little he would never hurt her.

"This is torture."

"Tell me about it," he mumbled.

Jonas helped her step out of the skirt. Smoothing his hands over her slender calves and skimming over the backs of her thighs, he hooked his fingers into her panties and tugged them down over the expanse of her honey-brown legs. She shuddered when he kissed the backs of her thighs. "Can you part your legs for me, sweetheart?"

She parted her legs a little.

"Wider." It came out as a harsh command.

She sucked in a breath and planted her feet about shoulder width apart.

Jonas trailed kisses up the backs of her legs, pausing only to nip at the backs of her knees. When he reached the top of her thighs, he ground out, "Lean forward for me."

It took her several moments to do as he instructed. When she did, he rewarded her with a soft kiss on her slick lips, and she shivered. Kneeling, Jonas lapped at her cleft and savored the unique spicy flavor that was JJ. With a hand on her firm ass, he massaged the skin as he teased her by sliding a finger inside her slick channel.

She cursed softly, but he continued his licking, and stroking, working his tongue over her clit while he slid two fingers inside her. The slick walls of her core milked at his fingers, and he felt them quicken. Kissing her inner thighs, he encouraged her. "Come on, JJ, come for me. You're safe. It's okay to let go. I'll catch you."

But she held on. She writhed against the door, and her slender hands balled into fists as she fought orgasm. She tensed as if she tried to fight one off, but then she went limp, and tossed her head back. Jonas continued to lick and stroke her until her whole body shook.

With a whisper of his name in the moonlight, she finally let go.

———

JJ shook as Jonas picked her up and laid her on the bed. Orgasm aftershocks rolled through her body, leaving her languid and foggy. What was he doing to her? And could she take more? If she wasn't careful, she was going to fall in love with him. Then where would she be?

He shed his clothes as if he was in no hurry at all, carefully unfastening his cuff links, then slowly unbuttoning his shirt. His slacks and boxer briefs came next. All the while, he kept his burning gaze on hers. Unable to take the intensity of his stare, she let her eyes drift closed.

His voice was soft, but authoritative. "JJ, look at me."

She shook her head.

His touch was soft on her cheek. "Shh, look at me."

She peeled her lids open to look up at him. "Jonas, I—"

"I'm not going anywhere. I'm right here with you. All you have to do is keep your eyes open to see it." He slid into bed beside her, and she had to scoot over to make room for him. "You with me?" He asked as he drew her close.

She nodded against his chest as she inhaled. Sandalwood. She sighed and immediately relaxed. She loved that smell.

Jonas pressed feather-light kisses along her temple, her forehead, her jaw line, the tip of her nose. When he reached her lips, he barely skimmed them with his own, and she whimpered. He angled his head and deepened the kiss and anchored her face in his hands as he devoured her lips. Desire spiked again as his expert tongue licked at the roof of her mouth, and he teased her tongue to follow into his hot mouth.

As she kissed him, she writhed against him, brushing her nipples against his chest, turning them into hardened peaks. His muffled moan made his chest rumble, and the friction against the sensitive peaks of her breasts sent a pull of desire straight to her core.

The length of his erection pressed into her thigh insistently, and she reached down to wrap her hand around the rigid length of it. Massaging.

"Jesus, Jessica."

With sure fingers, she continued stroking him, running her hand over his cock, her palm over the sensitive tip. When she did this twice, Jonas's hips jerked, and a drop of moisture escaped his erection to lubricate her palm. "Jonas. I want you again. I-I need you." Fear settled into her bones at that moment. If she needed him it would be a recipe for disaster, because at some point he would let her down.

"One of these days, you're going to have to learn to be patient."

A smile tugged at her lips. "It's not one of my virtues."

He growled low and kissed her deep. "I might have noticed." His fingers dipped between her thighs, and she shivered. When he slipped one impossibly long finger inside her slick heat, she moaned, parting her thighs to allow him better access.

"God, you are so wet. So ready."

"Mmm, Jonas." Lust rocked her body, and need chased the lust.

Jonas trailed kisses along her throat to her collarbone, moving to her breast. With his mouth poised over a distended peak, he paused. His breath tickled her skin, and she writhed. "Jonas, please."

"Please what?" His warm breath was a tease.

"Please kiss me."

He placed a kiss right above her breast. "Right there?"

JJ arched her back in frustration. "No. On my breast."

Jonas kissed the underside of her breast. "Oh, you mean here?"

"Damn it, Jonas." She threaded her hands through his hair. "Stop teasing me."

He kissed the underside of her other breast. "I like teasing you." He kissed her again and hovered over the tip of her breast again. "*You* like it when I tease you." Jonas used his thumb to circle her clit as he slid first one finger into her, then two. *Stroke, retreat, stroke, retreat.*

He kept the pace nice and easy, no matter how much she angled her hips, moving against his fingers. Finally, he withdrew his fingers and shifted position, brushing his lips over her nipple. "Jonas!"

"Yeah, JJ?"

He settled his lips around her nipple, and a pull of lust pierced her core. Jonas suckled her deep, his cheeks hollowing as he drew her into his mouth. Blood rushed in her head, and all she could think about was Jonas. His lips, his fingers. Like everything else in the world had vanished and all that mattered now was this moment, this time with him.

"I need you to fuck me. Please. I can't—"

"Who's in charge?" He grazed her nipple with his teeth.

"Oh, God. I—"

Jonas's fingers stopped penetrating her core. "Maybe I should ask you again. Who's in charge?"

"Jonas. Please. I—"

He removed his fingers from her heated skin and rolled his big body over hers, bracing himself over her. His erection nudged her cleft, and he swore. "You're so hot, JJ."

She rotated her hips, sliding her cleft along the length of him. "Jonas, please don't make me wait. I need you."

Jonas dropped his forehead to hers and kissed her softly. "All you have to do is relinquish control for a little while. I promise I'll give it back."

She chewed her bottom lip. The fear gnawed at her. The uncertainty eating her. He was too close. Could make her feel too much. He left her feeling open and vulnerable. He also left her feeling like she'd grabbed hold of a live wire. Like she could fly. Like she was beautiful. Like she was special. Worthy.

She dragged in a breath and exhaled. "You're in charge. I'm yours."

He kissed her softly before rolling away and pulling open the bedside drawer. Sheathing himself in a condom, he re-settled back between her thighs. "Do you know how long I've waited to hear that...that you're mine?" His tongue licked at her bottom lip before he nipped. "I'm not letting you go."

His erection slid against her slit before fully sliding into her. They both gasped. She met his gaze; his eyes pierced her soul. In that moment, she knew she would never be the same.

JJ met Jonas thrust for thrust. He kept his eyes on hers, never breaking the intimate connection as her orgasm coursed through her. JJ bucked as the pleasure rolled through her body. Jonas wrapped his arms around her and held on tight as his body shook.

CHAPTER FOURTEEN

They rested quietly together for a long time. JJ blinked sleepily, torn between wanting to drift into sleep with the thump of Jonas's heart beneath her ear and wanting to stay awake so she wouldn't miss a thing. Normally this was when she'd be looking for exit strategies. She'd always believed that keeping distance between her and the men she dated was best. Don't get too close or too attached. Strong emotion was too dangerous.

But this was different. Jonas was different. She couldn't have left him behind even if she tried. Not that she wanted to. This was bliss. Nothing had ever felt so good as losing all control in Jonas's arms.

"I want to take you out."

His voice came as a shock in the stillness, and JJ lifted her head slightly so she could see his eyes. There was a peace over him that made him look relaxed and glowing. Was that what she looked like too? Completely sated and happy? It was too much to hope for. JJ didn't want to examine her current state of happiness too closely for fear it would disappear in a puff of smoke.

"Take me out? Like, on a date?"

He grinned, his amusement obvious. "Yes on a date. Is that so hard to believe?"

She laughed. "Kind of. I'm so used to bickering with you and hanging out that it seems odd to go on a regular date."

Jonas's expression changed then, getting serious. "That's a mistake on my part. I've gone about this the wrong way. I want to take you out, Jessica Jones. You deserve that. I want to treat you the way a man treats his lady."

JJ shivered, inordinately pleased by the statement. He was looking at her like she was the most precious thing in the world. That was how he made her feel, too. Like she was this delicate thing that he wanted to protect and care for. She'd worked so hard to be independent and stand on her own two feet, that she'd never wanted a man to try to take care of her. What good did it do to look for that kind of treatment when most of those men only wanted one thing? Why get used to being taken care of when they weren't going to stick around for long anyway? But with Jonas, for the first time she had no fear that he couldn't come through. It was amazing how quickly he'd broken down her walls, but she did trust him, JJ realized with a shock. She absolutely trusted that Jonas was someone she could count on.

"What was that thought?" He brushed a knuckle over her cheek and it took all her power not to curl into the embrace like a kitten looking for a stroke.

"Just thinking about what a good man you are," she whispered. "You are so good to me. Even when I was giving you hell about everything."

His eyes lit up. "I hope you'll continue to give me hell. A man needs a woman who can keep him on his toes."

She giggled at that. He was deliberately being silly, but she found she liked it. He was always serious and it was wonderful to be the one who could bring out this lighter side of him.

"So does that mean you'll go out with me?"

JJ pretended to think about it. "Hmm, now that you mention it, I don't actually recall you asking me."

Jonas turned them over in one quick motion, making JJ shriek in surprise. "Okay brat. Here it is. Jessica Jones, will you do me the extreme honor of going out on a date with me?"

She curled an arm around his neck and pulled him down for a kiss. "Yes, I will. I would love to go on a date with you."

"Awesome! Let's go."

She raised an eyebrow. "Right now? Is this date clothing-optional?"

When she raised her hips slightly, Jonas groaned at the brush of her heat against his belly. "Now that you mention it, there are quite a few things I could show you right here in this bed first."

With a sigh, she sank back into the pillows as his lips took a detour down the side of her neck. His hands plumped her breasts, squeezing the soft globes gently. "I like that idea. But don't think you're getting out of taking me on a real date, mister."

"I wouldn't dream of it," he muttered. His voice was

muffled since his lips were busy tormenting the skin of her stomach. After one last nip, he scooted lower, propping her legs on his shoulders. He groaned when his lips made contact with her core. JJ bit her lip to hold back a cry at the first brush of his tongue on the super sensitive skin that was still recovering from the last few orgasms.

"Actually, maybe we can do the date thing tomorrow. I think we have a lot more work to do right here."

———

Waiting had become more difficult.

After getting the call, Matthias had changed clothes and then taken the scenic route to the meet, making sure he wasn't followed. It was easy to see if there was anyone tailing him at this time of night. Evasive maneuvers were as common to him as breathing. When you came from the streets, watching your back was second nature. Or at least it used to be.

Matthias kicked the dirt under his feet. He was restless. Or maybe just out of practice. He thought of the warm, spacious room he used back at Blake Security. The kitchen where there was always plenty of food and the common room where there was always someone to talk to.

He'd gotten soft and complacent after years of being comfortable. If the Matthias of ten years ago could see him now, he'd probably wonder who this slightly posh, slightly out-of-practice guy was. He wouldn't go soft though. He was never *that* comfortable.

Noah and the crew didn't mess around. The gym at the penthouse was state of the art, and he could lift more than ever with Oskar acting as his coach. It was just unusual to have weight on him after years of being so lean.

You didn't have a choice about being lean back then, he thought. Food had been a luxury he often couldn't afford.

A soft rustle told him he wasn't alone. He didn't bother to turn around. Sudden movements were never a wise choice in the circles he came from.

"You look different."

The voice was soft and the type that was hard to identify. Matthias knew that was deliberate. ORUS agents were trained to be as unidentifiable as possible. It had once been a point of pride for him that he could blend in, become invisible. It was only after he'd gotten a glimpse of what it could be like living as a free man that he'd known the desire to be seen. He'd gotten spoiled, living with people who treated him like he was different. Special.

The first time Lucia had looked at him like she trusted him, it made him believe that more might be possible for him.

Thoughts of her were always a problem, so he shook them off. He needed to keep his head in the game. You couldn't let down your guard around another ORUS agent. Not even one you called a friend. It was a good way to end up with a knife in your back.

"Hello to you, too. And what do you mean I look different? Do these pants make my arse look big? I thought black was supposed to be slimming."

"I'm not here to tell you any differently." The other voice held a hint of amusement now.

It was as good an opening as any. "So why are we here? It's not like you to call out of the blue."

"Someone has been digging."

Matthias cursed. "There's nothing for them to find."

A heartbeat of silence. They both knew that no matter how well you scrubbed information, there would always be something you missed. It was the nature of the beast. Matthias had always known that his past would rise up one day to haunt him. He'd just always assumed he'd have more time.

"Thanks for the warning, but I can handle myself."

"Yeah, I heard you took on Libra and lived to tell the tale."

Fucking hell. Noah wouldn't be happy about that. News about Rafe's miraculous return from the dead would surface eventually, but the rumor mill was working even faster than usual.

"Where did you hear that?"

There was a whisper of fabric. Shoulders shrugging? Matthias chanced a glance to his left. His old friend was wearing all black and his head was covered with a baseball cap pulled low over his eyes. *Nothing to see here.*

"I hear things. Word on the street is that you're coming back."

"The street can think whatever it wants," Matthias replied.

"Orion said you were coming back into the fold."

Now that was interesting. Was Ian really that delusional? Or maybe his newfound power was going to his head.

"You heard wrong."

He turned to walk away but stopped at the sound of his old friend's voice.

"Watch your back. Shit has been weird lately."

He nodded and then sped up his steps, eager to leave all remnants of his old life behind. He was never going back to that. He didn't care what Orion had up his sleeve.

CHAPTER FIFTEEN

O kay, so maybe she was giddy. Several weeks of good sex could do that for you.

So far by silent agreement, they hadn't told anyone. Though she was so sure any second now, they were gonna get busted. She did however feel guilty for not telling Lucia yet.

She wanted to tell her. Desperately. But she was also afraid of what would happen when the happy bubble burst. Would she revert to her old ways and run for the hills? Shit would get complicated if everyone knew.

Regardless of keeping that secret, JJ had a smile on her face and a spring in her step, but that was no reason for all the guys in the office to stare at her like she had two heads. Even the baby was looking at her funny. *No, she's not.*

But JJ couldn't help it. She was in a terrific mood. And yes, that was Jonas's fault. Not that she was complaining in the least. She usually wasn't one for PDA or people knowing her business, but this time she really didn't care. Besides, it was completely unavoidable.

And for a super spy undercover type Jonas was shit at hiding any of what was going on. They'd talked about it. About keeping the PDA to a minimum. About being careful. But it didn't stop him from staring at her. Or looking her up and down as if he wanted to lick her like a Popsicle.

Ooh a Popsicle. Yes please.

She really had to stop. But she couldn't help it. She'd insisted that they come in at different times this morning. Not like she wanted everyone knowing where she was last night. Or the last several nights really. She'd snuck in to her own room at three in the morning. And instead of him just coming in with her, he'd turned up at five, his usual time to use the gym. But instead of using the gym, he'd woken her up again with his mouth and *then* gone to work out. Devious man.

Over the breakfast table, Lucia eyed her suspiciously. And when Jonas walked by and pulled out her stool for her, Lucia's eyebrows popped. The moment Jonas was out of the kitchen, Lucia leaned forward. "You have some explaining to do."

"What?" First of all, she was a shitty liar. She'd never acquired the skill. Besides, this was Lucia. So lying directly to her face was nearly impossible. Lies of omission were simpler to pull off, but that required not seeing her best friend, which was kind of impossible since they lived together. "I don't know what you're talking about."

Lucia grinned, the smile going so wide she would probably split her lips soon. "For starters, you and Jonas are doing it. But where the hell are my details and gossip?"

"Would you keep it down?"

"Really? You two think you're hiding it? Everyone in this office has been watching the two of you fight like alley cats for years. All of a sudden he's pulling out your chair and looking at you like you're his favorite chocolate dessert and he doesn't want to miss an ounce."

"Look it's just—"

Lucia crossed her arms. "Follow me."

She gave Isabella a kiss on her cheek before handing her over to Noah in the living room. The baby cooed and clapped her little chubby hands together the moment she was in her father's arms. Noah grinned at his daughter as she proceeded to smack him in the nose with her little palm.

JJ snorted. She'd wanted to do that very same thing before. As she chuckled, she followed Lucia to her and Noah's bedroom, and then her best friend whirled on her.

"Spill. Start talking right the hell now."

JJ rocked back on her heels. "Um—"

"Don't bother lying; you're bad at it. Tell me everything. Best friend code right now."

"Fine. It's just I don't really know what's going on."

Lucia snorted through her nose. "I know what's going on. You and Jonas are boning. First of all, how is it? Second of all, please tell me it was everything. You two have been dancing around the last two years, so it had better be really, really good. Third of all, when? Fourth of all, how many times? Fifth of all, was this the reason you weren't home last night or most of this week and come to think of it last week? And the reason he's at the office extra early most mornings?"

JJ couldn't help but laugh. "Yes, fine. Okay—yes it happened a couple of weeks ago when everyone was freaking out because I decided to walk. I don't know. I've been feeling cooped up, I guess. I'm used to just doing whatever the hell I want, when I want. I mean the place is palatial, and I have everything I could ever need. I don't pay rent, and I don't pay for groceries, and I live in a fabulous penthouse, and my bedroom has a view of Central Park ... So it's heaven, right? But it's still a gilded prison."

Lucia nodded. "Yeah. I know. I hear you. Sometimes it can feel like that. But remember everyone is only worried about your safety. We've had a lot happen to the team, and I couldn't bear it if something happened to you."

JJ took her hand and then joined her on the edge of the bed. "I know. And I am grateful. I mean God damn it, I had a fire in my apartment. And you guys have been generous enough to let me stay. I do not mean to complain at all, I swear. It's just, I'm not used to having roommates, so it's an adjustment. So anyway, I wanted to walk home, get some fresh air. Jonas found me of course—he was being Jonas."

Lucia chuckled. "Yes, of course, he was being Jonas."

JJ left out the part about thinking someone was following her. "Yeah, so he pulled up, and of course he was shouting at me. And I don't know what happened. Well, I do know actually. We kissed. That was the first time."

"Yeah, you told me that part. So what happened next? How did it progress? I feel like I need popcorn for this."

JJ rolled her eyes. "I don't know. Something spooked me one day when I was running errands for the office. Like you said, a lot has happened in the last year, and I swear I was seeing things. Then, I don't know, I was really freaked out. I called Jonas for pickup and he came and got me, and took me to his place because I didn't want to come back here and have to explain to everyone how I was freaking out over nothing. And everything was fine, and I just wanted to take a minute to breathe. And then the next thing I know, I'm jumping his bones."

Lucia's mouth dropped open. "You *jumped* him?"

"Please don't remind me. It was humiliating enough at the moment."

"Wait, he turned you down?"

She nodded. "Yep, #turnedallofthisdown."

Lucia scowled despite JJ's attempt to be humorous. "He's a moron."

"Yes, I'd have to agree. I was pissed." Again, she left out the nitty-gritty details of the humiliation. And she left out the part about her desperation move. The need to try and block out the unpleasant memories with sex. Lucia didn't need to know all that.

"So, we came home, and I was in a mood. Irritated, ticked off, horny. And he followed me, and of course we were fighting as usual. And then he pretty much asked me if I was okay because he said I wasn't acting like myself. Which was bullshit." *Liar*.

"Aww, Jonas can care sometimes. He can really be very sweet."

"Weren't you just calling him an idiot a second ago?"

Lucia shrugged. "He's just like his best friend. One moment in my good graces, the next moment I want to slap him."

"I know this feeling well," JJ laughed. "So anyway, he's being all extra sweet, and then I'm losing it because I feel rejected and like a crazy person, and then he kisses me. And then we, uh, and then we boned."

Lucia whooped. "Fantastic. Wait, where the hell were we? Somehow everyone seems to know when Noah and I are having sex."

"You guys were out. And I'm pretty sure Matthias knows. I'm not exactly quiet. But then I also didn't want a big deal made. You know me. Next week I could run. So we've been keeping it quiet ... sort of."

Lucia clutched her belly and giggled. "Man, that poor kid. We are traumatizing him for life. Do you know how many times he's walked in on me and Noah?"

JJ held up a hand. "I don't want to know."

"No, you don't."

"Yeah, so that's it."

"No, that is not it. Because sex is one thing, but then what happened after that?"

"Not much. I mean we still had to work. So in the middle of the night, he left my bed, grabbed his stuff and went home. Came to work the next morning like everything was normal. But then after work, he came to pick me up. That was last night. He took me to his place and made me dinner."

Lucia's slow smile warmed JJ up from the heart. "Oh boy. This is going to be a thing isn't it?"

"Do not get excited."

Why not? You're getting excited. What if this could be real? She shoved that thought down immediately.

"I don't know if this is gonna stick. Right now it's good sex. And good food. Two of my favorite things. And obviously you know what he looks like, so huge ego boost."

"You're being ridiculous. He's the lucky one. Okay, so he made you dinner and then you guys ... "

"Well, it's very hard to keep my hands off that man. I'll just say that."

"Oh boy, you guys are gonna fall in love. I can tell. I can feel it."

JJ wanted to be excited. But she knew Lucia didn't have all the details. Lucia didn't know why she kept herself at arms length from most men. Lucia didn't know why Jonas wouldn't be sticking around forever. Lucia didn't know her deep and dark hidden secrets. So all her best friend could see was the happiness and potential. The problem was, on the course she was on, either she was going to get hurt or Jonas was. And Lucia and the rest of the team were going to get caught in the middle.

———

He was nervous.

You have no reason to be nervous. You've already slept with her. Twice. This is just a date.

Except this wasn't *just* a date. He liked her. *You've always liked her.* Yeah, he had always liked her. Well, mostly he had wanted to shake her and sleep with her. But liked her? Not exactly. He'd always respected the fuck out of her. She was strong. Sexy. Smart. Kept him on his toes, which was awesome and annoying all at the same time.

Yeah, he'd always liked her. But somehow, it felt like he needed to do this right. Because there were so many ways that this could go wrong. And he didn't want it to go wrong.

And now, everyone knew. *Mostly because you can't help but stare at her.* Yeah, that was it. Twice during their debriefing meeting this morning, he'd been so busy staring out the glass window at JJ walking by that Noah had to snap his fingers in front of his face. When Jonas had snapped out of it, all the guys had been looking at him with shit-eating grins on their faces. Fuck them all. He didn't care.

Yeah you do. Because you know how this will affect everyone if this shit goes wrong.

This was true. But given that they were grown-ups they could probably manage it. *Who the hell are you kidding? You'll go back to fighting like cats and dogs and actually hate each other.* Fuck, he really hoped that didn't happen. Because he had a feeling he'd be thinking about tasting her for the rest of his damn life.

He knocked on her door and she opened it with a wide smile. "What is all this?"

"This," he spun around adjusting his jacket and deliberately showing off, "is your date for the evening. Go get changed. Something sexy and flirty. You look gorgeous in red."

She paled. What was that about? Then just as quickly, she shook her head and smiled slightly. Jonas wasn't sure what he'd said that could cause that reaction. Maybe she was feeling a little bashful remembering wearing nothing but his red tie last night.

"And just where would I be going in this red, sexy, flirty dress?"

"Can't tell you that. It's a surprise. Come on, get changed. We're going to be late."

He loved that happy, surprised grin that flashed over her face. He wanted to put that grin there all the time. Fuck, he had it so bad. This was going to end in disaster if he wasn't careful. *Slow it down. Don't overwhelm her.* This was supposed to be easy, fun, not too serious. He had to repeat that over and over again until his brain started to remember.

When she came back out, she'd opted for red and black. Fine by him. She still looked amazing; the dress tied at her neck, leaving most of her back exposed. Which meant he could touch as much as he wanted.

"You look—wow."

She grinned. "Oh, this old thing?"

"Come on. Let's go before everyone notices we're all dressed up."

With a giggle, she followed him through the path of least resistance, which meant from her bedroom, through the kitchen, completely avoiding the living room, gym area, and conference room. They snuck out the door, but not before Oskar called out, "You two kids have fun now. Jonas, remember to bring her back at a reasonable hour. And if you two are gonna get up to extracurricular activities, please warn the rest of us so we can wear our earmuffs. I don't think Matthias has recovered after the other day."

Jonas groaned. He was going to fucking kill the German.

But JJ didn't miss a beat. "You guys can go eat a bowl of dicks, you hear me?"

A bark of laughter choked out of Jonas and he stared at her. "A bowl of dicks?"

She nodded "Yep, I'm going with it."

"Woman, you are ridiculous."

She danced into the elevator. "Yep, but that's why you love me."

He knew she was kidding. She was being flippant. She did not mean that. *But it's not untrue.* Oh shit. He was tripping over the landmines of his feelings. Because he *was* falling for her. Even though he could see the collision toward disaster. He didn't care.

Once they were in the car heading toward the Met, she turned to face him. "A car service? My, my, Jonas Castillo giving over control? I must ask what is happening here."

"You and I both know I give you control. But I figured this way we could have some fun, and be irresponsible and not have to worry about driving anywhere. So relax. We're on a date."

"I love how all our dates thus far consist of you telling me what we're going to be doing."

He shrugged. "I see no problem with this."

"Well, hold onto your britches because I will plan a date for you, and it's going to be something you don't expect."

"I look forward to it."

He took her to a show at the Met. And admittedly the show wasn't all pleasure. It was also to do a check-in on a client whose husband had been more paranoid as of late. She'd come into the office to ask for additional protection and the team set up surveillance on her. But last week she called asking them to call it off. The event at the Met was mostly a welfare check on a would-have-been client. But after that, everything was all JJ.

The Met was featuring a lesser-known opera. And it was

short; only an exhibition to get everyone to buy tickets to the big show. And of course there was the party after. But they weren't staying for that.

Mrs. Elliot Anderson looked none too pleased to see him. But still, she was cordial and introduced him and JJ around. When he managed to get her alone for a moment, she said, "I told you; I made a mistake coming to Blake Security. I'm not in danger."

"I understand what you're saying. At the same time, I just want to be sure. Sometimes people say things on the phone if they're being coerced. So we like to do a welfare check in an environment where they don't expect us. More difficult to lie this way. But you're fine?"

She nodded. "Yes, absolutely." Jonas could see the lines of tension around her mouth. This woman was *not* okay. But he was learning to maybe let go a little bit. Of course he'd send Dylan or Ryan to follow her and sit on her place. But he couldn't force her to want their protection.

Once he was done with her, he found JJ chatting with an artist near the bar. The guy was laughing, reaching out a hand and caressing JJ's arm. That had Jonas frowning immediately. *Mine.* Yeah, that constant thought, that was gonna have to stop, too. She would not like being referred to as his. Still, he had to maneuver her away from the handsy artist.

He strode right up to her, leaned down, and nuzzled her neck. "You ready to go sweetheart? I want to feed you."

She turned into him with a happy smile. "You said my favorite words. When she'd bid the guy goodbye and they were halfway to the door, she turned to him. "Don't think I don't know what you were doing."

"And don't think I won't stake my claim. I want you. He was trying to poach. I didn't appreciate it."

"So you peed all over me?"

Again, the unexpected laugh. "Seriously? I mean, if you're into that ... "

"Eww. I am not. But someone's feeling very territorial tonight."

"Of course I am. I'm here with the most beautiful woman in the room."

The rest of the night, Jonas couldn't remember when he'd had this much fun. He took her dancing. A little salsa, a little merengue. They were a little overdressed, but man, was it fun. And true to his word, he kept her well fed.

The classic Mediterranean place he'd taken her to had a Michelin starred chef. And JJ squealed when she saw where they were going.

"I've been trying to get a table here for a year."

"I aim to please."

After dinner, once they were headed back to the car, he slid an arm around her before leaning down to gently brush his lips over hers. "So princess, your place or mine?"

"Aren't you being a little presumptuous?"

He laughed. "Hell yes. And I promise you sweetheart, I'm a sure thing."

"In that case, I'm yours."

"All right. Get your asses in gear. We have a lot to do today." Noah rubbed his hands together and the room quieted.

Jonas, however, had his eyes on the man sitting on Noah's left. It wasn't unusual for them to have outsiders in the office, but considering who the guests were, they were all on edge. He could see it in the hard set of Oskar's shoulders and the tense lines around Matthias's mouth. Ryan and Dylan didn't know the history Noah and the others had with ORUS, but even they could tell something was up. It wasn't often they had Ian, the head of ORUS, sitting in on their meetings.

"First up, lets do a status check on our current clients. Jonas, how are things with Lindsey Meyers?"

While he went over the details of his last check-in with Lindsey, Jonas kept one eye on the man who'd accompanied Ian. David. The guy was pretending to pay attention, but every so often, his eyes would slip to the windows leading out into the main office area. What the hell was he looking at? Jonas coughed and turned discreetly, checking to see if Lucia was walking around or something. Hell, if the dude got caught checking out Lucia they wouldn't have to worry about a probationary period. Noah would take him out before he even got started.

"Also Rafe is coming in a little later."

"Excellent. We need all the help we can get. Ok, I'll turn the floor over to Ian. He and one of his best agents have been working on a case for the past few months that they need assistance with."

As Ian stood to speak, Jonas kept his eyes on the man still sitting. What was it about the guy that rubbed him the wrong way? Maybe it was the shit-eating smirk on his face, like he knew something they didn't, or was just tolerating being here.

When Noah had told them about Ian's unusual request for them to assist on a case, he hadn't minced words. He didn't like the idea of getting into bed with ORUS, even if it was only temporary. Also, the agent assigned to this particular case, David West, code name *Chamaeleon*, had been a little too trigger happy back in the day, in Noah's opinion. Matthias hadn't said anything, but Jonas definitely got the impression he didn't like the guy either. Still, considering how valuable it could to be to have the head of ORUS owing them a favor, he couldn't blame Noah for taking the case.

"Thanks for the help, Noah. This is a time sensitive situation. We might need significant technical assistance on this one." Ian glanced over at Matthias, who didn't move.

Movement behind him caught Jonas's eye again. David had shifted in his seat slightly and was staring out into the main living area. Jonas barely heard Ian droning on about rebel strongholds in Colombia because his senses were tingling. Something was up with this David guy, and he was going to figure out what it was.

Noah dropped into the seat next to him. "What's your take on this?"

He was used to Noah asking for his read on all types of situations. Coming from law enforcement, he had the training to detect liars and the general gut instinct to tell when shit was about to get real. But he wasn't entirely sure what to tell his old friend. Ian was Ian, no surprise there. The real wild card was David West, who was only here to assist Ian. So why did the guy make Jonas so anxious?

"What's the deal with that guy?" He inclined his head slightly in David's direction.

Noah snorted under his breath. "Your typical over-confident ORUS agent. I remember him. He was always hanging around me and Rafe, trying to one-up us. Not exactly a team player. I don't know why Ian brought him in on this."

"Is he always this twitchy? He acts like anything could set him off."

Noah's eyes narrowed as he took in David's rapt attention to something outside the room. Finally Jonas turned again. Lucia stood right outside in full view, laughing at something. The room was soundproofed so they couldn't hear her, but it was pretty obvious what David was staring at.

"Motherfucker." Noah stood, his chair scraping back from the table loudly. Everyone stopped what they were doing and looked at him. Jonas figured he had about two seconds to defuse the situation before Noah went nuclear.

"Gentlemen, we've just gotten word of an emergency situation. Apologies, but we're going to have to cut this short."

Without waiting for another word, Matthias stood and walked toward the door. Ryan and Dylan glanced around in confusion.

"This is time sensitive," Ian began.

Noah held up his hand. "Let's go to my office. Ian, why don't you and David come with me? Jonas can handle this situation while we finish up."

Jonas smirked. He wasn't sure how he was supposed to handle getting Lucia out of sight, but he'd have to think of something. Hell, maybe he'd just tell her the truth. She knew better than anyone how jealous Noah could be. Luckily she loved him madly and put up with him and his crazy ways.

"That's fine." Ian looked confused but followed Noah's lead. David walked up right behind him. To Jonas's surprise, Noah stuck out his hand.

"David. It's been a long time. How long have you been

back stateside?"

The other man winced slightly, and Jonas looked down to where Noah had his hand locked in a vice grip. "About six months," David finally ground out.

Jesus. He needed to get them out of there before Noah decided to go all He-Man and challenge the guy to a duel or something.

"I'll start handling the emergency situation," Jonas said.

Noah smiled at him gratefully. "Thank you. I'll call you when we're done."

Translation: Don't bring Lucia back here until this motherfucker is gone.

Jonas smiled. "Got it, boss."

He walked out of the office and was immediately able to see what Lucia had been laughing at. JJ was in the kitchen, just out of view, holding up a picture of something on her phone. His heart sped up when he saw her.

"Hey baby. I didn't even know you were back yet. That didn't take long."

She shrugged. "I couldn't find anything. Shopping isn't as much fun without Lucia. So I figured I'd wait until you guys could watch the baby so we can go. I need her to tell me which tops make my boobs look the best."

"I can do that," Jonas promised.

"Yeah, I bet you can."

Damn, this was fun. As much fun as their bickering had always been, it had partially been born of sexual frustration. How amazing was it to have this back and forth chemistry with a woman who satisfied him completely in every way? Jessica Jones was truly his perfect match.

It hit him like a lightning bolt. She was the one. His future. His destiny.

His wife.

Jonas almost fell to his knees at the intensity of the thought. Marriage had always been something that he figured he'd avoid. It wasn't as if he'd had the best exposure to the institution, and truthfully, he'd never understood the point of a piece of paper when you could just live with whomever you wanted. It wasn't like it was the 1950s and you'd get run out of town for living in sin.

But in that moment, Jonas got it. He understood Noah's obsession with having Lucia as his wife. He wanted the same things with JJ. He wanted her to be his. To carry his name. To be filled with his child. He wanted them merged and blended in every way possible because he knew without a shadow of a doubt that he was meant to be with this woman forever.

"I can so do that," he mumbled, reeling from the life-altering thoughts going through his head. The entire land-scape of his future had just realigned in the space of a heartbeat, but the rest of the world went on unaware.

JJ smiled at him gently. "Did you hear anything I just said?"

"No," he answered truthfully. "I was too busy wondering how I got so lucky that you're mine."

———

She opened her mouth but no sound came out. Everything became background noise. Lucia telling them how sweet they were, the rumble of Noah's voice, and even the sound of her feet on the floor as she walked over to Jonas. None of it registered in light of the heart-stopping look on his face.

"I feel exactly the same way."

The way his eyes crinkled as he smiled made her so warm

inside. It was amazing how making him happy could complete her. But over the last few weeks, she'd slowly discovered that the formula for her ultimate happiness lay in Jonas smiling at her exactly like that.

"I love you, Jonas."

His arms opened automatically and she cuddled into his embrace. She stood on tiptoe and pressed her lips to his. He swallowed the little whimper she made and cupped her cheek to hold her still as he devoured her lips.

This was home, coming into his arms and knowing that she'd always be welcome there. It was more than she'd ever dared to hope for, but here it was. Living proof that dreams could come true.

Then, right before her eyes, it all turned to dust.

Because standing right behind the living embodiment of her dreams, was the ghost of the man who'd once torn them all down.

"No. It's not possible. No. No. No."

With a cry, JJ spun on her heel and ran from the room, dropping her phone in the process. She heard a chorus of voices calling after her but she didn't stop. She couldn't stop. His face swam in her mind, and she ran faster. She had to get to safety.

Where the hell could she go? Then she noticed the door to Noah and Lucia's room was ajar. She pushed it open, her eyes sweeping the room. Her gaze landed on the flat wall across from the door.

The panic room.

Noah had made her and Lucia practice the code over and over when she'd first moved in. He'd claimed that muscle memory would come through for them in an emergency even if they were too rattled to remember the code. As her fingers raced over the buttons, JJ promised to thank him later. The door slid open and she rushed inside. She didn't take another breath until the door slid closed behind her.

"Jesus, what the hell?" The muffled voice from outside the door made JJ whimper.

How had he found her? She went to the far corner of the small room and curled up in a ball on the floor. After so many years, just when she thought she was safe.

Haven't you learned by now? Nowhere is safe.

JJ covered her head with her arms and sobbed.

CHAPTER SEVENTEEN

Jonas ran his hands over his face. She was in the panic room? What the hell? It took a few minutes for his brain to start working amidst the adrenaline rush of chasing after her. He glanced behind him. Lucia had followed and stood hovering in the doorway.

"Where is she?" Lucia asked. Her eyes darted around the room and she held a hand to her chest as she panted for breath. A second later, Noah appeared in the doorway next to her.

He pointed to the wall across from them. It took a few seconds before she got it. Lucia's eyes widened.

"She's in the panic room?" Her eyes followed the same

path his did to the blank panel on the wall.

"It appears so. What was going on before I saw you guys? Was she behaving strangely?"

Lucia rubbed her arms. "No. She was totally fine. I mean, she was bitching about not fitting into any of the clothes she liked. But that's the usual. Then she was talking about getting one of you guys to babysit Isabella so we could go shopping together. That's when you came out. This doesn't make any sense." Lucia bit her bottom lip. "She was totally fine. We were talking the whole time you guys were having your meeting. What changed?"

Jonas walked up to the wall. "JJ. Baby, it's me. Are you okay?" He listened intently. Nothing. Then he heard a soft sob. "I'm coming in."

"No! Don't come in. Don't let him in!"

Jonas glanced behind him at Lucia who looked just as perplexed as he felt.

"What is going on?"

Lucia shrugged. "I honestly have no idea. She was so happy to see you just a few minutes ago. I don't understand why she doesn't want to see you all of a sudden."

Jonas flinched. What could he have done that scared her this badly? He mentally reviewed everything that had just happened. She'd looked so happy to see him and maybe he'd been a little aggressive with that kiss, but he'd just had a major epiphany. Had he scared her off with his intensity?

JJ wasn't keen on the idea of forever any more than he'd once been. Maybe it had been too much, too soon? It was a blow to think that the idea of forever with him was enough to send JJ literally running from the room, but he knew her fears and her past. She'd had valid reasons not to trust and not to hope for more. But slowly, every day, he was going to show her what was possible. It was his new mission in life to teach her how to love without fear. Hell, he'd be teaching himself along the way too. Because this shit was terrifying already.

He knocked on the door again. "JJ, baby you know this room is only for emergencies. I know you're mad at me but you don't need to hide in the panic room. I'm coming in now, okay?"

The only response was another round of heartrending cries. She sounded like she was barely breathing. Jonas cursed. Her sobs tore at his heart. Had he really done this? But nothing else made sense. Although she probably wanted privacy, he couldn't take it anymore. He typed in the code and when the door slid open, his heart broke all over again when he saw JJ curled up on the floor in the corner.

Then she raised her head, and his blood ran cold. JJ looked completely terrified and not entirely aware of where she was. This wasn't about her being angry at him. Something had happened. He'd seen this kind of thing before in some of their clients, especially the ones who'd been abused. Something would trigger a memory, and then they'd react like they were right back in their personal hell.

"Lucia, it's okay. I've got this. Go tell the others not to disturb us please."

"Of course." Lucia patted his arm before leaving with one last worried glance back at her friend.

Jonas ducked his head to enter the room. It was about ten feet by ten feet and painted stark white. Not designed for comfort, for sure. JJ couldn't be comfortable all crunched up in a ball like that. He sat next to her and then scooted as close as he could without touching her.

"JJ, I'm so sorry. I don't know what I did to scare you but I'd never want to hurt you in a million years."

She turned suddenly and threw herself into his arms. Relieved that she wasn't running away from him anymore, Jonas held her, allowing her to sob into his shoulder. It was about ten solid minutes before she quieted. The only way he knew she was still awake was the shaky gasps of her breathing.

"He was right there. Right there in front of me. I haven't seen him in so long."

Suddenly she bolted upright. "Oh my God. He's out there with Lucia! I have to warn her. I have to get her away from him."

"Whoa. Hold on baby. Warn Lucia about who?"

"David," she cried. "I have to warn her about David! What if he hurts her or the baby? I was so scared I just ran. What kind of friend am I?"

Holy fuck.

"JJ, are you saying you recognized David West? That you know him?"

He sat up straighter, the events of the last hour racing through his mind. David's intense concentration on something in the common area. He hadn't even seemed to care about what Ian was saying. Jonas had thought he was looking at Lucia because she had been the one visible to him, but had he been looking at JJ the whole time? She wouldn't have been able to see him since they'd had the tint on the conference room windows turned on, preventing anyone from looking in.

She nodded miserably. "He's ... he's the one. Jonas, he's the one who hurt me. The guy I told you about."

"Son of a bitch." Jonas pulled his phone from his pocket and sent a quick text to Noah and Matthias. Hopefully they could read it without tipping off David or Ian.

His phone rang a few seconds later.

"What the fuck is going on?"

"I guess that means they're already gone. Damn it!"

JJ flinched next to him, and Jonas reined in his temper. He couldn't let his anger touch her. She'd had enough of violence and fear.

Noah's voice was tight. "You need to explain. Why should I have detained them?"

"Give me two seconds. I'm going to get JJ out of here first, and I'll come find you. Can you have Lucia meet us? I think JJ could use a friend right now."

He knew that Noah understood what he meant. While Lucia took care of JJ, he and Noah would come up with a plan to take care of that fucker David West.

Take care of him permanently.

———

He was carrying her.

Under any other circumstances, JJ would have more than a few snarky things to say about Jonas carrying her around. But honestly, after her little crying fit, she wasn't entirely sure she even had the strength to stand. After he'd made arrangements with Noah over the phone, he'd wiped the tears from her face with the kind of gentleness she hadn't known he possessed, and then he'd scooped her up in his arms. She'd rested her head on his shoulder and let him carry her to his room.

She'd expected to feel ridiculous, letting a man cart her around like she didn't have two perfectly working legs of her own, but instead she'd felt cared for and protected.

The way David once made you feel. Look where that got you.

Because the thought brought back the vague sense of panic, she pushed it away. She wasn't going to think about that. Noah and the guys were handling it, and she trusted that they wouldn't let him anywhere near her. Now that the first rush of panic had passed, her brain could approach the problem in a rational way. She was no longer the scared, young teenage girl who hadn't had the will to stand up to David. She was a strong, independent woman who knew her own mind. He couldn't manipulate her if she didn't allow it.

Those days were over.

JJ curled up on Jonas's bed, burying her face in his pillow. His scent enveloped her, surrounding her with a sense of safety and comfort. After her crying jag, she felt like a dishrag that had been wrung out to dry, but she took a deep breath. Despite being older and hopefully wiser, she could still acknowledge the pull the past had on her. It had been an emotional gut punch to see David in the flesh for the first time in so long. She'd reacted with the instinct of the scared girl she'd once been. But she was okay.

Everything was going to be okay.

Then she remembered that despite not being a scared kid anymore, she was still only human, and David was still violent and unpredictable. He'd been standing only a few feet from her and people that she cared about. What if he'd hurt Lucia? Saying that things were okay might be a bit of a stretch.

"JJ, can I come in?"

She sat up at the sound of Lucia's voice. Her friend's head appeared in the doorway. She glanced around the room uncertainly.

"It's okay. You can come in." She waved her friend in and scooted over so Lucia could sit next to her on the bed.

They sat in uncomfortable silence for a few moments before Lucia spoke. "Jonas just told me that you knew that guy. That he hurt you."

JJ's eyes filled with tears. She could only imagine what her friend must be thinking. She'd kept secrets, and those secrets had put Lucia and her family in danger. She hung her head.

"I'm sorry I never told you."

That seemed to break the distance between them. Lucia sat on the edge of the bed and grabbed her hand.

"This isn't about hurt feelings. I just want to make sure

you're okay. You have the right to tell whomever you want about it. Or to never talk about it at all if that's what you want."

Relief that her friend wasn't angry flooded through her. JJ squeezed Lucia's hand. "I didn't want to talk about it. I just wanted to forget it happened."

Lucia paused. She looked uncomfortable. It wasn't often that they didn't know what to say to each other. They'd been friends so long that they were both used to speaking without a filter.

"You don't have to be careful with me, Lucia. I'm really okay, despite my little breakdown in there. We've never minced words with each other. Let's not start now."

Lucia smiled softly, but it was strained. "I'm just so sorry someone hurt you. And that I wasn't there to help out when it happened."

"You were there. You've always been there. I was the one who kept it a secret. I didn't know how to admit that I was in trouble."

Lucia stretched out on the bed next to her. It reminded JJ of when they were teenagers and would have sleepovers and stay up all night talking. Back then, they'd giggled all night about what their lives would one day be like. If they'd get married and have a husband and kids of their own. What it would be like to have a man who adored them and did all the wicked things JJ read about in her mom's romance novels.

But after Rafe died, things had changed for both of them. Lucia had lost her beloved brother and become a shell of her former self. JJ had lost her best friend, and she'd been desperate to feel … something. Rafe's death had been a blow to her too, for many reasons. Not just because of how it affected Lucia but because he'd been her first crush. It had been a shocking introduction to the concept of death to so suddenly lose the first man who'd ever made her feel like a woman.

Not that she'd ever told Lucia any of that.

"How did you meet him?"

JJ thought back. The moment would forever be emblazoned in her mind.

"He saved me, actually. There was this guy hassling me on the street. Wouldn't let me walk by. David just looked at the guy and he backed down. I thought it was so romantic back then, but looking back, I wonder if that wasn't my first warning sign. If criminals are afraid of you ..."

"But there was no way you could have known that then," Lucia protested. "You've always been smart about guys. You were never the type to jump into things."

"Everything was so crazy then. With Rafe gone, everything was different. And David was so nice to me at first. He made me feel special. He said he wanted to protect me."

Lucia sniffled. "How could I have not noticed that my best friend needed me? We were together all the time."

"Don't you dare blame yourself. You had enough to deal with grieving and taking care of Nonna. You just figured I was spending time with my boyfriend."

"A boyfriend who was hurting you." Lucia's voice sounded tortured.

"He always said that he'd never let me go. God, Lucia I believed him too. I never understood why he left me alone one day. It was so sudden, but all I could do was be grateful. Then I felt so guilty because more than likely the only reason he left me alone was because he'd found someone else to torment."

"That isn't your fault. He's the sick bastard, and Noah and the guys are going to kick his ass when they find him."

JJ closed her eyes. She didn't want the guys to go after him. At one time, maybe that would have been what she craved. Revenge. But now all she wanted was for everyone to be safe. For things to go back to normal. To have that perfect life she'd started to believe was possible.

"I love Jonas so much," she whispered.

"I know you do. He loves you the same way, I can tell." Lucia's eyes shone with glee. "You have to know how thrilled I am to see you guys together. He's the type of guy you deserve, JJ. A good guy."

But as they drifted off to sleep together, JJ couldn't help but wonder if that was really the kind of guy she deserved.

CHAPTER EIGHTEEN

"I will fucking kill him."

It turned out that expression, 'seeing red,' was a legit real thing. Jonas had never been so angry in his fucking life. He marched right past Oskar and Matthias, past the gym and straight for the weapons room. Noah was hot on his heels.

"Jonas, whatever's going on man, back down."

He turned on his friend. "Back down? Are you out of your fucking mind? That asshole is a psychopath." He wasn't sure how much to say to Noah. But with Lucia in with JJ, Noah was going to know anyway. And they had a real fucking security problem now.

His friend frowned. "Dude, tell me what the fuck is going on. I've only ever seen you like this once. Talk me through it."

Matthias had been right behind Noah. And Oskar had followed them. Rafe lingered somewhere in the doorway, somehow still separate from the main group. "Ian's body-guard. Chamaeleon? That animal used to stalk JJ. He—hurt her."

Noah frowned. "What?"

Matthias got his time-to-start-killing-people face going. Rafe stood straighter and cracked his neck. Jonas had started to recognize that as his kicking-ass face. Oskar was the only one who stayed calm, leaning against the wall. But when he spoke, his voice was quiet and deadly. Jonas had learned that when pushed, Oskar could be far more dangerous than any of them. And that included Rafe.

"Explain, Jonas," the German said quietly.

"I guess they used to date. That's when it started. He beat her. Stalked her. Made her feel weak." They would know the whole story eventually when JJ decided to tell it. Right now he gave them the bare bones minimum.

Noah frowned across his arms. "I'll give Ian a call."

"No, you won't give Ian a call. I don't want to give that asshole any knowledge that I'm coming for him."

"Not without me," Matthias said.

Rafe just nodded his head. He was always down for an ass whooping.

Noah shook his head. "No. No one's going in for an ass kicking. We need the full story first."

Jonas listened, but he still armed himself with pistols, made sure that he had extra magazines, and grabbed one of the shotguns too. Just for shits and giggles. What he needed was a rocket launcher. Yes, he could blow up anything with a rocket launcher. He knew they had one in here somewhere. Where had Noah put that?

"Jonas, talk to me."

Jonas stopped and turned around. "There's personal stuff for JJ to tell you. All you need to know is that asshole is not a good dude. He hurt her. From what she told me, he'd been gone for a long time. But he's back now. Which means that she's in trouble. The last few days she's been feeling like something was off. I bet you anything it's that jackoff."

Noah nodded. "Look, you know no matter what happens,

I have your back. And we *all* have JJ's back." The guys all nodded. "But Chamaeleon is one of Ian's guys. This is no run-of-the-mill asshole we can pluck off the street, scare straight, and hand off to the cops. We need to be careful. So we'll talk to JJ, and we'll bide our time. Going in weapons hot like this is only going to get you or one of the other guys killed."

That took a little wind out of his sails. He didn't want the team anywhere near this. "I don't want anyone dying for me. I'll do this one alone."

He tried to brush past Noah, but his friend didn't budge even an inch. *Asshole.* He glared at Noah and Noah glared right back. "Jonas, I've told you this before. You want to fight, we'll fight. You want to work off some steam, I'm your guy. But I'm not going to let you walk into your own death. If this guy's been stalking JJ this long, he's not going to fight fair."

"Neither am I."

"Yeah, but there's a difference between you and that guy. At the core," Noah thumped him on the chest just over his heart, "you're a human being. You don't kill for fun or for sport. On the job, you rarely fire your weapon. That guy, he's a born and bred killer. That's what he is. And if he's dumb enough to hurt someone like JJ, that means that he's the lowest of the low. He will kill you and anyone else who gets in his way for nothing. And I'm not losing any of my guys. We're going to do this smart, do you hear me? Because JJ is going to need you."

Motherfucker. Noah fought dirty. *Because, he was right.* JJ would need him. She needed him now. If he ran off after this asshole, she would be all alone tonight. And she deserved better than that. His shoulders sagged, and he let one of the pistols fall into his palm. Gingerly, Matthias came forward and took it from his hands. He ensured the safety was on, and removed all the ammunition. Piece by piece, his boys took all the guns from him. Even his personal piece. Noah took that one.

When he growled at his friend, Noah held up both hands. "Sorry man. You'll get this back in the morning when you're more level headed, you hear me?"

Yeah, maybe Noah had a point. This way, he couldn't wake up in the middle of the night with a penchant for murder. That wouldn't be good for JJ.

"I hear you. But just so we're clear, that asshole dies, right?"

Matthias and Rafe nodded immediately. The thought of

killing didn't turn their stomachs. What surprised him was that Oskar and Noah nodded as well. Noah had never taken to the life of an assassin very well. It had always eaten at him a little. And Oskar. Oskar hadn't been an assassin like the other three. But when it came to protecting women and children, he erred on the side of killing the assholes and asking questions later.

"Yeah, okay. I'm gonna go see JJ."

Noah clapped him on the back. "I think that's a good idea. You'll do her more good being with her than going off half-cocked."

———

There was a knock at her door and JJ lifted her head to find Jonas in the doorway. "Hey you."

His voice was soft, but she could sense the turmoil in him. He nearly vibrated with it. "How you feeling?"

"Tired. Raw. Like I scraped the scab off of a healing wound with a dull rusty blade."

He smirked. "You've always had a way of painting a picture. You got room in there for one more?"

She nodded and scooted aside in her bed, alarmed at how much she needed him. When Jonas reached the bed, he gently tucked her hair behind her ear, and then stripped off his own clothes.

Unmistakable heat flashed between her thighs, and she couldn't help a smile. Sliding in beside her, Jonas tucked her against him so they spooned with his hand cupping her breast.

"Jonas, what—"

"I'm going to hold you, if that's okay. You know how much I want you." He dragged in a sharp breath when she wiggled her ass against his thick erection. "Hell, you can feel it." His cock twitched against her ass. He clearly wanted her, but all he did was continue to hold her. "I need to hold you more than I need to make love to you. If that's okay."

She nodded then whispered, "Thank you for today."

Jonas kissed her ear softly. "You have nothing to thank me for. I'm not going anywhere."

It was in the cocoon of his arms that she was finally able to fall asleep.

Hours later, with streaks of moonlight casting shadows

into her room, JJ moaned into Jonas's chest. She was awake enough to know she was having either the very best of dreams or one hell of a wakeup call. Jonas kissed her as his thumb and forefinger rolled one of her nipples. Sighing into the caress, she let herself relax into the kiss. His expert tongue caressed and teased hers into playing.

God, she relished what he could do to her body. The way he made her pliant. He never rushed her, even when she wanted to hurry. He always took his time with everything, even kissing her, like they had all the time in the world. Like his erection wasn't straining.

She loved kissing him. His lips were so soft and skilled, and his tongue—every time he licked into her mouth, it made her shiver. When his hand dipped between her thighs, she parted them to ease his way. Skilled fingers stroked her cleft, teasing her, driving her crazy. She arched her back trying to angle her hips into his hand.

Jonas slid a finger inside her as his thumb caressed her clit and she cried out and sank her fingers into his hair. He grunted in satisfaction as her hips bucked, then he sucked on her tongue in time with his fingers sliding into her slick center. His heavy erection continued to press into her thigh and she moaned. She would never get over what he could do to her body. She'd never been so carnal, so aroused, so willing to give herself completely to anyone.

With a groan, he pulled back from their kiss and she mewled as she tried to follow his lips. His gaze scorched her. Dark and fiery, he stared at her under hooded lids. "Jesus, what are you doing to me?"

Her constricted throat made it impossible to speak, so she responded the only way she knew how—by arching her hips into his hand again.

He muttered a soft curse, and squeezed his eyes shut. As his fingers strummed her to the edge of orgasm, he chewed on his bottom lip. When he increased the pace of his questing fingers, JJ held tight onto his shoulders. She rotated her hips around and around until he swore again and rubbed his thumb directly over her clit.

Her orgasm ripped through her, laying waste to every nerve and cell. Unable to think, she threw her head back giving herself over fully to the sensation.

"Holy fuck, you are so beautiful when you come."

She smiled up at him, expecting him go for a condom, but instead, he burrowed under the covers. His hands parting her thighs had her tensing. "Jonas, I–"

He tugged the sheet down and lifted his head. After he crawled back up her body, he turned her chin firmly so she was looking at him. His gaze burned hot, the desire etched on his face was unmistakable. "Do you trust me?"

JJ nodded. "Of course."

"Good. Now I'm going to erase every memory of that asshole from your body. I will erase every memory of any other man before me. Tasting you is one of the highlights of my day."

"I-uh..." Wow. "In that case, who am I to stand between a man and his mission."

"There's my girl." His smile was lopsided. "Look at us sharing control."

He slid back down her body, placing kisses across her chest and belly as he went. When he reached her hips, he nibbled at the flesh on her pelvic bone, then scooted still lower.

Dusting feather light kisses on her inner thighs, he paused when he got to her cleft. "So pretty. And so soft." His first stroke of her slick center had her clenching her hands into the sheets. Oh God. He lapped at her, kissing her and exploring her with his tongue. He took his time, as he did with everything else. He seemed in no hurry. When his tongue circled the throbbing bundle of nerves, JJ flew apart in his hands again. But he didn't let up. He kept stroking her. Kept lapping at her.

It wasn't until he slid a finger into her moist sheath again that she lost all her inhibitions. Forgot everything she'd been afraid of. Forgot the shadows that had been chasing her and gave herself over. If he was intent on killing her with ecstasy, then who the hell was she to argue?

Finally relaxing, she let her thighs fall apart and he moaned, parting her folds and dipping the tip of his finger into her center. Her third orgasm rolled through her, chasing the tail of the previous one, he didn't let up until she lay limp.

He drew himself back up her body, pausing to nip at her hips again, then to suckle her breasts.

When he made it to her lips, he said, "I'm going to make that a new daily habit."

She shivered. He could do that to her any time he wanted. "God, yes."

He shifted against her parting thighs with his. And she moaned when the tip of his erection nudged her cleft.

He squeezed his eyes shut tight as he entered her inch by inch. JJ met him halfway by raising her hips. His jaw stayed tight until he was seated all the way inside her. He made love to her sweetly. Kissing her, holding her to him and looking into her eyes. "You're mine. And I am yours."

In that moment, the fear fell away. This was the perfect moment, the one she'd always looked for. This was the kind of love and acceptance she'd been seeking all her life. "I know." Blissful abandon started in her toes and cascaded through her body. She held onto him tight and muttered how much she loved him as the orgasm took over all her conscious and subconscious thought.

As her body held him inside her, he whispered in her ear, "I am so lucky." With two more deep strokes, his whole body shook with release.

CHAPTER NINETEEN

"Y̶ou know you can't save the day every day, right?"

Jonas looked up from his post at the floor-to-ceiling windows. He'd left a sleeping JJ to think this shit through. Besides, if he'd stayed, he'd have made love to her again. Marked her as his ... again. He hated that someone had hurt her, that that jackoff had bruised that beautiful body.

Noah braced his arms in the doorjamb and studied him.

"Yeah, I know."

"Trust me. Above all else, I understand the run-in-and-kill-it compulsion when the woman you love is in danger."

"I know that, Noah. I just can't help it. I want to be out there. *To find him.*"

"I know. And I get it. But first of all, that's not you. You are the law-and-order guy; the justice guy. He's a prick. And very likely deserves to go home in a body bag. And that's what we'll do. But you know why I can't let you go off all renegade. This is not a Rambo movie."

"I just need to fix this for her. She is afraid, and there is nothing I can do. Do you have any idea what that feels like?"

Noah fixed him with a slanted glare. "Have we met?"

Jonas shook his head. "Yeah, I know. I know you know. I just—" He sagged against the window. "Is it supposed to fucking feel like this?"

"You mean that feeling of being totally out of control, when the only person you ever cared about this deeply is the one person you don't know how to protect?"

"Yeah. That feeling."

"Yeah, it's called love."

"I mean, this is JJ. She's brash, and bold, and doesn't need anyone. On any given Sunday she's telling this lot over here, a den of killers, to go suck a bowl of dicks. More often than not she doesn't listen, she does not temper her emotions, and fucking hell is that woman loud."

Noah grinned. "Yeah, we've heard."

Jonas glared at him. "You know, we all had to endure you and Lucia, attempting to sneak around but doing a shit job of it. So JJ likes to scream." He shrugged. "I'm not going to stop the woman."

Noah put up his hands. "I'm not saying you should. It's just, well, we have a sleeping baby most of the time."

Jonas rolled his eyes. "Shut the fuck up."

Noah chuckled low. "Yeah, I hear you. Look, we're a team. We do things together. We go in together, always. That is how we stay alive. That is how we keep JJ alive. JJ, Lucia, Isabella, each other. Not one of us gets to go off on our own. We've all seen how poorly that ends up."

"I love her," Jonas whispered, finally giving himself permission to say the words. Some of the tension coiled tightly in the center of his chest eased. He did love her. All he wanted was her. Safe. That was it. Even if their shit didn't work out, and God, he hoped it did, but he still just wanted her happiness most of all. *Then keep her alive.*

Noah smirked. "Yeah, I was wondering when you were going to get around to that."

Jonas chuckled. "Did everyone in this office think we were going to get together?"

Noah snorted a laugh. "What? You didn't think so? Because I could pretty much see where this was heading the moment you first laid eyes on her. You were completely gob smacked, standing there with your mouth open, catching flies and shit." His chuckle deepened. "I will never forget it. JJ strolled right up to you and said—"

Jonas didn't even let him finish before quoting JJ himself. "'Yeah, I get this reaction a lot.'" He shook his head. "She was so full of herself. Seriously. I just wanted to shake her. And kiss her. Which irritated me even more."

His friend's shoulders shook with mirth. "I know, man. She's a handful. And she deserves someone as good as you. So for once in your life, listen to me. We will get this asshole. But we will do it together, and we will do it smart. No one is going to touch her. This is our family. And we protect what's ours. We'll figure out what's going on with ORUS. What they're up to. And we'll get retribution for JJ. But first, we watch them. We study what they're doing. We keep this shit methodical. Then we move."

Jonas nodded. "And then we kill the bastard."

Noah nodded. "Yeah, that too."

———

This was all JJ's fault. Every single man in this penthouse was in total kill mode. Now, while some of that was kind of hot, she didn't want this kind of fuss just for her. This had not been her intention. *But what are you gonna do? Tell them not to protect you?* These guys, however frustrating they were at times, were her family. Which meant they would protect her with their lives. Not that she wanted that, but she knew them well enough to know that they would not listen.

"You guys, thank you for rallying the troops and all that. Especially since I have a penchant for telling you to go suck on a bowl of dicks. I appreciate it."

Matthias shook his head. "Don't mention it, love. We're family. We stick together."

His words were soft. But he was nearly as scary as Rafe

with the look he had in his eye. JJ didn't have all the details, but she knew that Matthias, Rafe, and Noah were not your garden-variety security folks. First clue were those tats that they sported on the backs of their necks and their wrists. They were all different, but extremely similar. To the casual observer, they were just a clustering of dots. Maybe freckles? But Lucia had told her once they were tattoos and refused to tell her anything else. Truth be told, she had a feeling that she didn't really want to know. Although, she really *did* want to know. But these were the kind of secrets she had a feeling would get someone killed. So she kept her mouth shut.

Regardless, Noah was the least scary of the crew. He was mostly charming and happy-go-lucky. Unless it came to Lucia, and then the man went insane. He would do anything to protect her.

Rafe, by contrast, was serious. *All the time* serious. He rarely joked. The smiles were few, unless he was holding Isabella. Or talking to Lucia or Nonna. He had a few smiles for her too, but he didn't say much.

JJ had a feeling his seriousness had everything to do with whatever the hell had caused him to fake his own death. Again, it was one of those things that no one talked about.

She was personally just happy to have Rafe back in their lives. And happy to see her friend get her brother back.

Rafe had tried to kill Noah and the other guys at Blake Security last year, so pretty much no one talked about that time. Except Oskar. Oskar brought it up as often as possible. Always poking and needling Rafe. She was secretly terrified that a proper fight would break out one of these days.

And then there was Matthias. Yes, he could be scary. Especially when he looked like this. But mostly, he was sweet ... as sweet as a British, tattooed, hacker-type could be. As far as she knew, he didn't do as much of the personal security work. He was more on the tech side. Whenever he did do security though, he got this look on his face. Like he'd beat anyone who even considered getting in his way. And when he looked like this, it was scary shit. He looked almost as lethal as Rafe did.

She wasn't an idiot though. All three of them were lethal. She just didn't want to ask if they had any practical experience.

"Thanks for saying that Matthias. You guys are the best family a girl could ask for. But seriously, this whole place has a Debbie Downer mood on it. You guys should go out. I get it; Jonas will be my bodyguard."

Oskar snorted. "Yeah, we all know how he guards your body."

JJ flipped him off. "Seriously, though. Noah, take Lucia out of here. She's worried. And it's not good for Isabella. You guys go with Rafe. Jonas and I will stay and babysit."

To her surprise, Jonas nodded his agreement, even though Isabella was known for just smacking him in the face whenever he held her. She did it with such glee and a giggle, like it was her favorite activity. And she also had a penchant for vomiting on him. But still, he volunteered for babysitting duty.

"She's right. You guys go out. We'll stay here. Keep an eye on things."

Noah shook his head. "No one's going anywhere. We're all staying here until we get the lay of the land."

Matthias threw up his hands. "I swear to God, you lot act like a bunch of old biddies. I have eyes on Chamaeleon. JJ is safe. No one is going to let him near her. Why don't the lot of you go out? Lucia, you call the nanny. I'll stay and keep eyes on things. And that way,

JJ, you get out too. Jonas, if I have to look at your dour face for another minute, I'm likely to stab you in the chest. So all of you go. Leave the baby with me. It's not like I don't know how to change little love's diapers by now."

JJ giggled. No one was sure what it was about Matthias. But every single time someone handed him the baby, Isabella gave him a nice warm diaper. So he had a lot of practice changing her by now.

Oskar tsked from the corner. "Does you wanting us out of here have anything to do with your crush on Katie the babysitter?"

Poor Matthias. A flush crept up his neck even as he glowered at Oskar. "Shut it."

Of course that just made Oskar laugh harder.

Lucia stepped forward and put her arm around JJ. "What do you think? Can you try and forget about things for a night and let us cheer you up? We'll have Noah and Jonas and Oskar, and I assume we'll be taking Ryan and Dylan as well. Rafe begged off, said he needed to crash. We'll have a night out. Most of the gang."

JJ slid Jonas a look, and he nodded at her.

"I don't know. I just feel like you guys will be all worried and tense, and I don't want anyone to feel like that."

Lucia just gave her a tight squeeze. "Come on. We're going out. Go get some sexy heels on and make these men buy us drinks and chocolate desserts, and maybe even makeup. You know how Oskar just loves spending an hour in Sephora while I look for just the right shade of lipstick."

From the corner Oskar moaned. "Please don't. Anything but that."

JJ grinned. "I'm having fun already. Okay. If you guys are sure."

Jonas came over and kissed her on the forehead. "Go get changed. We'll work out some security protocols. We'll go have some fun and attack the problem in the morning, okay?"

She nodded. When she gazed up at him her heart squeezed. "I love you. You know that."

His smile was slow and confident. "Oh I know. You've been in love with me for years." He nodded sagely as she rolled her eyes. "Which suits me fine since I knew I wanted you from the first moment you opened that sassy mouth of yours. So let's go out. We deserve to have some fun."

"You got it. I have just the backless dress and fuck me shoes for this occasion."

He groaned low. "I swear, you're trying to kill me."

JJ grinned up at him, feeling light for the first time since David showed up. "What a way to go."

CHAPTER TWENTY

I am a truly lucky man, Jonas thought to himself as he watched JJ make her way around the dance floor. When she noticed him watching her, her eyes heated and she sent him a sultry wink. He shifted in his seat, chuckling softly at the power she held over him. The woman could tempt a monk to sin with nothing more than a look.

Earlier that evening, she'd made a comment after shopping with Lucia about being all dressed up with no place to go. She'd been joking, but the words had cut through Jonas like a knife. No matter what was going on, he never wanted JJ to feel that he was keeping her locked up, away from the world. It was always going to be a challenge to temper his need to protect her and keep her safe, with her need to be free. But that was love, wasn't it? Balancing your own needs with the one you cared for. Giving up certain things to gain something far more precious?

It was astounding what he was willing to give up if it meant days and nights with JJ by his side.

She caught his eye from across the room, and immediately her lips curled up into a soft, secret smile. He loved that smile. It always seemed like she was plotting something or up to some mischief. Which wasn't ever far from reality. She was dancing with Lucia and both women were dressed to impress with silky gowns that enhanced curves and had the power to make a man forget his own name. As he glanced over at Noah, he knew his friend felt the same way. They had found the dream.

"They're teasing us," Jonas mumbled.

Lucia had her eyes closed and was swinging her hips, in a world all her own, probably unaware that her husband was on the verge of knocking the heads off all the men currently ogling her. JJ, on the other hand, was completely aware that she was driving Jonas crazy, and she loved it. The little vixen watched him through hooded eyes as she danced, then executed a shimmy that almost made him come in his pants. He reached beneath the table and discreetly adjusted himself, thankful that the long tablecloth gave him some privacy. It was bad enough that he had Oskar and the rest of the guys ribbing him about how whipped he was already. The last thing he needed was to give them more ammunition. Not that he really cared.

Besides, they were just jealous. He could understand. If he had to watch someone else with JJ, he would be jealous as all hell, too. Just the thought made him grind his teeth.

Jonas cursed when he noticed a guy sidling closer to the girls. Then the man turned and met his gaze. Jonas's eyes must have communicated his intentions because the other man suddenly turned and walked the other way.

Jonas chuckled. He wasn't fooling himself that he was that powerful. No doubt it was Noah, Oskar, Ryan and Dylan also glaring at him that did the trick. He was lucky to have a crew that loved her almost as much as he did.

"It's been a long time since we went out like this," Noah commented. "It's good to get out. I'm surprised Lucia hasn't said something before."

"There's been so much going on. But things are finally settling down now. It's time we start living our lives. Hell, maybe JJ and I will have a few babies so Isabella has someone to play with."

Noah chuckled. "Look at you, all domestic and shit. I would have never thought I'd see the day you were playing house with a woman."

Jonas sat back in his chair, the idea settling in his mind like it had always been there. It would have scared the hell out of him a year ago to talk this way, but then he glanced over at JJ again and it just felt ... right. She was his and there wasn't a single doubt in his mind about that. The thought of being with her forever wasn't scary at all. Hell, he never knew what the crazy woman would do next, so it wasn't like he'd ever be bored.

"She's worth it."

Noah clapped him on the back. "That she is. She's a handful though, so kudos to you for being man enough to handle her."

"I'm sure he doesn't mind handling her at all," Ryan commented with a little grin. He dodged the punch Jonas threw his way easily. "No disrespect intended. It's just awfully hard to be around couples who can't keep their hands off each other. I thought Noah and Lucia were bad. I know you guys thought you were keeping it on the down-low when you started hooking up, but you guys are the worst secret shaggers known to mankind."

Oskar snorted. "At least they kept it to his office."

Jonas winced. "Geez. A guy gets caught with his pants down in the hallway one time ... "

"Twice," Dylan corrected. "And you tried to play it off like you just happened to lose your trousers on the way to the bathroom."

"Pretty sure it was more than that," Oskar said. "There was the time when we ordered Chinese and then that Saturday morning when they woke up Isabella. Then the time when they sneaked off in the middle of movie night. It was a Star Wars marathon, too. Some people have no appreciation."

"Wasn't there a laundry room incident?" Ryan added.

"Okay! I get it." Jonas ignored their laughter. "You'd better not say anything to JJ about this. I don't want you goons embarrassing her."

Suddenly JJ plopped down in the seat next to him, bringing the fresh sunshine scent that was uniquely her own. "Tell JJ what?"

"About how much you and Casanova here are boning in the office," Oskar drawled.

Jonas groaned and dropped his face into his hands. If he wasn't built like a brick wall, Oskar wouldn't get away with half of the shit he said and did. He could only hope JJ wouldn't get offended or think he was talking about their sex life behind her back. But before he could even respond, JJ slid a hand into his lap, perilously close to his dick.

"Well, maybe if you could lay the pipe like he does, you'd be getting some in the office, too!"

The guys all dissolved into laughter at the stunned look on Oskar's face. Jonas knew his mouth was hanging open but couldn't seem to gain control of it until JJ patted his cheek.

"Everything okay, Casanova?" Her eyes sparkled as she teased him.

Jonas turned so his lips brushed over her forehead. "Perfect. Everything is perfect. And so are you. I love that smart mouth of yours."

"And so do we," Ryan chimed in, still laughing. "Anyone that can put Oskar in his place has my vote."

Lucia was snuggled into Noah's lap, and the rest of the guys looked relaxed and happy. At least as relaxed as any of them ever were. But it was a good reminder that no matter how much they went through, they'd always have each other's backs. Blake Security was their family and Jonas was grateful for it.

"Let's go home. Maybe we can bone in the laundry room again. The smell of detergent turns me on now."

JJ covered his mouth with her hand. "You are a sick, sick man."

"Oh, that's going too far?" he asked incredulously.

The entire group was in great spirits as Noah paid the check and they walked out to the parking garage. Jonas opened the door for JJ, and she hopped up in the cab of the SUV. A loud yawn burst from her lips and she giggled.

"Damn. I used to tease Lucia about not being able to hang. All this boning with you has worn me clean out," she teased.

He leaned into the interior of the vehicle to kiss her. "I'll put you to bed as soon as we get home, Miss Jones."

"Promise?" The erotic gleam in her eyes had Jonas

rounding the vehicle much faster than usual to get to the driver's side.

———

JJ watched as the lights and familiar buildings of Manhattan rushed by. She was tired, it was true, but more than that, she was content. As much fun as it had been to take a night out for dinner and dancing, she was excited to be at home with her man.

Her man.

She smiled to herself at the private glee the thought of Jonas always brought to her. After so many years believing that being alone was the only way to be independent, it was a bit of a shock to discover that not only did she enjoy sharing her life with a man, but she was coming to need him. Jonas had proven himself and his intentions. No matter what went down, she trusted him to be there for her with no questions. After what had happened with David ...

JJ shivered. She couldn't pretend that it didn't worry her to know that he was still out there. It was a bit of a mind fuck actually, to have this mental image of him walking around New York, able to show up and scare her at any moment. But she was assured that Noah and the guys were on it, and with Matthias tracking him, it wouldn't be long until he was located. They had told her that he was an ORUS agent, so he knew how to hide, but even an agent could only remain underground for so long. Once he poked his head out of whatever hellhole he was hiding in, they'd have him. The whole time she'd dated him she thought he was a bouncer at a Manhattan nightclub.

And she doubted they'd be turning him over to the authorities.

"What are you thinking about over there?" Jonas asked. He couldn't keep his eyes on her face since he was driving, but she could still see his worry in the crinkle of his brow, even in profile.

She definitely couldn't tell him her thoughts. They'd made a pact to be honest with each other and she took that seriously, but there were some things that would only bring him torment. Telling him that she was worried about David would only make him feel guilty that he hadn't been able to protect her. No matter how many times she'd told him it was ridiculous, he carried guilt over that. Apparently Jonas thought he was superhuman and could foresee the future. But JJ knew the truth, which was that sometimes life was a bitch and just threw curveballs to keep you hopping. It wasn't anyone's fault; it was just the way of things. She didn't want him beating himself up over her past mistakes coming back to haunt her.

He'd shared more with her about his mother, his memories, and his greatest regrets. JJ had listened, comforted and cried more than a few tears over the fate of a gentle woman who'd wanted nothing more than to be loved. Jonas would always have a certain sense of responsibility to protect the women in his life because of his past. She knew that and accepted it, even when his overprotectiveness drove her up the wall.

"JJ. Everything okay?" Jonas glanced at her again.

She cleared her throat. "I'm fine. Just thinking about everything that's happened."

At his scowl, she reached over and squeezed the hand that wasn't on the steering wheel. "I know you guys are taking care of things. But I can't wait until it's all over. I don't want any of you getting hurt because of me."

Jonas picked up her hand and brought it to his mouth. The brush of his lips over her skin brought to mind a litany of erotic images. Scenes she knew they'd be acting out as soon as they got back home.

"There's only one person who's going to get hurt in this scenario. And that's David West. Or whatever his real name is."

JJ sat back abruptly. His real name. It shouldn't have been such a shock to hear the name he'd been using was an alias, but somehow it was. How strange that a man who'd had such a profound effect on her life and her distrust of men, probably wasn't even who she thought he was.

Sensing her distress, Jonas pasted on a smile that didn't quite reach his eyes. "I shouldn't have said anything. We've got this. Okay?"

They rode the rest of the way back to Blake Security in silence, each lost in their own thoughts. By the time they pulled into the underground garage, Noah and Lucia were already out of their vehicle waiting for them. Her friend had already lost most of the baby weight and now just looked like a curvy pinup due to her new motherhood-enhanced chest. They'd been shopping earlier, and every one of the tops and dresses Lucia had chosen displayed quite a bit of that chest.

JJ smiled at the thought. Lucia had been waiting her whole life to have cleavage. She could hardly fault her for flaunting it now, although if the look on Noah's face was any indication, he wasn't enjoying the thought of anyone else seeing it.

Lucia put her arm through JJ's and hugged her close. Her friend's eyes were slightly glassy. After abstaining from alcohol since getting pregnant with Isabella, she'd lost the little bit of alcohol tolerance she'd once had.

"I had so much fun tonight," JJ told her. "And I can tell you did, too."

Lucia grinned. "Yes, I did. After eating that delicious meal and not worrying about the calories and having a glass of wine, I'm going upstairs to rock my hubby's world!"

There was a snort of laughter from behind them. JJ turned just in time to see Noah smack Oskar on the back of the head.

"Well, before we lose you, do you mind if I come with you to check on Isabella? I need my baby fix."

Playtime with her favorite almost-niece was one of her favorite things. She'd been down for bed before they left so JJ hadn't had a chance to play with her. It hadn't escaped her notice that Jonas adored Isabella as well.

Every time she saw him holding the baby, her imagination went crazy with images of him holding their child.

She placed a hand on her stomach. It was almost too much to imagine. Being with Jonas forever. Having his baby. A sudden sense of unease swept through her, making JJ shiver. It seemed like too much to hope for. Like she was tempting fate.

"Of course. Izzy loves you." Lucia presented her face and held still for the retinal scanner and they moved to the back to wait for the rest of the guys to get on the elevator. Once they arrived at the penthouse, they all went their separate ways with a chorus of *good nights* sounding behind them.

"I'm just going to kiss Isabella good night," JJ said.

Jonas smiled. "I'll come with you. This is good practice for us. For one day."

Even though it mirrored her earlier thoughts, it was a thrill to hear him say it. JJ grabbed his hand and dragged him behind her. Noah and Lucia trailed behind them.

"It's so quiet in here. Usually Matthias would stick his head out to say hi or something."

Jonas shrugged. "He's been in a mood lately. Probably just doesn't feel up to making conversation."

JJ wasn't so sure about that. Matthias had been plenty chatty before they left, all smiles for the babysitter. Katie was a sweet girl, working her way through college toward a degree in sociology. Not who she'd have expected to ring Matthias's bells, but whatever. She was happy for him. Everyone should be in love.

Well, just look at me, she thought. *A regular Hallmark card.*

She turned the doorknob to the nursery and took a deep breath of the soft baby powder scent that perfumed the air no matter the time of day. It was almost midnight, so she hoped the baby would be sleeping soundly and wouldn't even notice them. The curtains were drawn, so the room was dark save for the small princess nightlight near the bed.

JJ tiptoed forward, stopping next to the crib. The room was decorated in all the frilly, lacy things that Lucia loved. It was like a Disney cartoon threw up in there. But for safety reasons, there were never any pillows or blankets in the crib itself. Noah had been even worse than Lucia in drilling the safety rules into all of their heads.

Blankets, pillows and sheets were a suffocation hazard for infants.

Which was why JJ was puzzled to see that the baby was swaddled heavily in blankets.

"Lucia, did you tell Katie to swaddle the baby?" Immediately she reached into the crib to pick up Isabella. She wasn't sure why Katie would have done that when she knew the rules better than any of them. Noah had chosen carefully from a list of potential babysitters and they all had been experienced in childcare and CPR certified.

Lucia moved to her side. "No, of course not."

"Well, she did. I don't know what she was thinking." JJ pulled back the first layer of the blanket. When the baby's face was revealed, her blood instantly turned to ice.

"Oh my God."

She turned around. Lucia, Jonas, and Noah watched her in confusion. Later, she'd wonder how she'd kept breathing when her heart had stopped beating.

"What's wrong?" Lucia asked. Then she saw the baby's face.

And screamed.

"Isabella? Where is Isabella?"

She snatched at the doll in JJ's arms, examining it as if it would magically transform into her beloved daughter.

Tears spilled from JJ's eyes as she scanned the room frantically. Noah already had his phone to his ear barking out orders. Jonas approached her slowly, before putting his hand gently on her shoulders.

"I don't understand what's happened. Where's Isabella? Why would Katie put a doll in her crib?"

His eyes were heartbreakingly kind as he pulled her into his embrace. JJ let out a soft moan as she took her first deep breath in what felt like ages.

"She wouldn't," Jonas said quietly. "Oskar just called. He found Matthias in the living room unresponsive. Katie's gone. And so is Isabella."

JJ pulled back slightly. "Why would she do this? Money?"

"I don't know the answer to that, but we are going to find her. You can believe that."

Lucia's wails sounded from behind them, and JJ's heart broke for her friend. That someone could hurt an innocent child ... It was chilling.

The baby doll lay on the ground at their feet, forgotten. JJ picked it up, mainly to make sure Lucia didn't have to lay eyes on it again. It was a standard doll, with a small wisp of dark hair on top and big blue eyes. However, someone had painted the lips a bright crimson red. She touched the lips and her fingers came away smeared with lipstick.

I've always loved you in red.

The memory slammed into her as crisp and clear as if it had just happened. David loved for her to wear lip color but he had particularly loved it when she wore red lipstick.

JJ turned to Jonas, clutching the macabre doll to her chest. "He was never really gone, was he?"

Jonas pulled her close and kissed the top of her head. "Who, sweetheart?"

"David," she murmured.

"We've had all our contacts watching out for Chamaeleon. You don't need to worry. You're safe," he promised.

But JJ had gotten the message. Loud and clear. She wasn't safe and she never had been.

And neither were the people she loved.

———

We hope you enjoyed *Force*! Ready to find out who took Isabella and how the Blake Security crew gets her back? **One-click *Enforce* now!**

Or get it at malonesquared.com/force

Turn the page for a sneak peek at *Enforce*!

Numb terror.

That's all JJ felt. She was so angry and worried and sick she couldn't even move, breathe, or speak. Someone had taken Isabella right from her home. "This is all my fault. It had to have been David."

Jonas rubbed her back in slow circles. "This has nothing to

do with you. This has to do with *us*. All of us. They want a war, they've got one."

JJ turned into Jonas's arms and her gaze flickered up to his. "I wish it was that simple. You don't understand. *This* is what he does. He terrorizes everyone around you so that you're completely alone. So that no one will want to be with you. So that you're a pariah. I wish I could say he's the kind of man who wouldn't hurt a baby just to fuck with me. But he would."

Jonas held her tight. "We're not going to let that happen. I promise. We're going to get Isabella back."

A sob racked her body. What was she supposed to do? How was she supposed to fix this? She had brought pain to her friends. Into her family. Once her parents moved away to Florida to be closer to their friends, she had no one else. These guys were the only family she had. And because of her, Noah and Lucia's baby was gone.

From the couch Matthias groaned, and Noah ran to him. "Kid?" Noah shook him hard and slapped his face. "Kid, wake up."

Matthias groaned some more, and even in his sluggish, obviously drugged state, he managed to defend against some of Noah's assaults. JJ was pretty sure she would've just lain there like a rag.

When Noah slapped him again, Matthias caught his arm, cranked it under his own, and then raised his other hand to hit him in the face. But then he blinked rapidly and realized who he was about to hit and released Noah. "Blimey. Pretty sure the fucking twat drugged me. What the fuck?" He tried to sit up, but Noah shoved him back down.

"Easy. We don't know what she gave you yet. Doc's on his way to take your blood and will rush some lab results."

Matthias shook him off. "I'm all right. Just a fucking bitch of a headache." And then he let out a slew of curses that JJ could only assume came from a lifetime rolling about the streets of London. When he pushed himself into a sitting position, Lucia went to him and kneeled in front of him, holding his hands.

"Matthias, do you remember anything? Anything at all? They took Isabella."

Matthias's brows snapped down and he stared at Lucia hard. "The baby? Fucking cunt took the baby?"

His gaze darted to Noah whose expression was grim and his jaw set. But he nodded. "Yeah, they took the babysitter too."

Matthias shook his head, and then groaned loudly as he cradled it gently with both hands. "Nah, mate, no one took her. She brought me a drink. Said she made tea. Fucking Earl Grey. I was downed because I wanted a spot of tea. That is so fucking bullshit."

Lucia shook her head. "But I vetted Katie. *You* vetted Katie. We all did."

It was true. The nanny had been interviewed by every single member of Blake Security. They'd dug through her background, her past boyfriends, any roommates she had. They'd gone over her financial records. That babysitter pretty much had top-secret clearance at this point with all the background checks she'd had.

"I know." Matthias said. "But it was her. No one else could've accessed or bypassed the biometric scanner or the alarms. Unless those were on when you guys came in."

Next to JJ, Jonas stiffened. "No. No alarms. Our phones didn't go off either. Nothing."

Matthias cursed again. "Yeah. It was Katie then because no one else could have gotten in here."

"Kid, you feeling up to it? We need to access the security feed to see what happened, and you're the only one who can do that quickly," Noah said.

"Fuck. You've been waiting for me to wake up? We're losing time." He pushed to his feet and swayed, and Noah shoved him back down into a sitting position. "You stay here. Oskar, run and bring the kid his laptop."

JJ had never seen the German run so fast. But he was back in less than a minute and handed the laptop to Matthias. Matthias's fingers tapped over the keyboard at such a fast rate she could barely see the individual strokes he was making. "Yeah, mate. Here she is; bloody cunt is in the kitchen making the tea." He turned the laptop around, but when they all couldn't see it he made another few quick taps, and the security footage appeared on the television set. He pointed. "Yeah, there she is, putting whatever it is in the tea. And then she brings it in here to me. I was working on something. But Isabella refused to sleep, so I had her one-handed, you know. Like you do sometimes, Noah, so that she can see outward and play a little, and then she falls asleep."

Noah's lips twitched, and he blinked back tears. "Yeah, I know."

Matthias sniffed too. "Fuck mate. I'm so fucking sorry. I'm such a fucking idiot. I took the tea. I drank it. Didn't taste any different, didn't smell any different."

Noah shook his head. "This isn't on you. This is on her. We just need to see the rest of the video."

Matthias fast-forwarded the video to show what happened when his head started to nod back. Katie took the baby, and then she made one call. "Yes. He's out." She was silent for a beat, and then her gaze darted to Matthias and back to the baby. "I don't think I can do that. If that's what you want to happen, you'll have to come and do it yourself. Because I won't. I told you that already."

"Is there any way we can track who she was talking to?" Jonas asked.

Matthias frowned. "I might be able to hack her phone. Pinpoint her location. Read her text messages. But without the actual physical phone, it will be next to impossible to determine who she called. I'm fucking sorry. This is on me."

JJ stepped out of the comfort of Jonas's arms. "No Matthias. I've already taken the blame. It's because of me that all of you are in this position. He wants me. That's why he took her. Because he knows it would hurt me to see all of you hurting. Matthias this wasn't your fault. We'll find Katie. If anyone can do it, you can."

Lucia nodded. "JJ's right. You would be the one who could find her."

"I'll do my best. Again, I'm so fucking sorry."

"Don't be sorry. This wasn't you. Just find her," Noah said.

Lucia stood and turned to JJ. "Look, I know you blame yourself, JJ. I actually blame myself for leaving. I know Noah's gonna rip himself apart. And Matthias, you're killing yourself because you drank tea. None of us are to blame. The person to blame is this Chamaeleon character. He and Katie. We blame *them*. And now we all have to band together and bring my daughter home."

Noah wrapped his arms around her. "Lucia's right. We are a family. We won't crumble. And together, we're going to find my daughter. Even if it means taking the fight straight to ORUS. We *will* get her back."

Matthias tried to stand again but thought better of it. "That's just the thing you guys. I'm not entirely sure ORUS is behind this."

One-click Enforce now!

M. MALONE is a 2019 RITA® Award winner and a NYT & USA Today Bestselling author of completely inappropriate romantic comedy. She spends most days wearing Wonder Woman leggings and T-shirts that she's embarrassed for anyone to see while she plays with her imaginary friends.

She lives with her husband and their two sons in the picturesque mountains of Northern Virginia even though she is afraid of insects, birds, butterflies and other humans.

She also holds a Master's degree in Business from a prestigious college that would no doubt be scandalized at how she's using her expensive education. **minxmalone.com**

USA Today Bestselling Author, **NANA MALONE**'s love of all things romance and adventure started with a tattered romantic suspense she borrowed from her cousin on a sultry summer afternoon in Ghana at a precocious thirteen. She's been in love with kick butt heroines ever since.

With her overactive imagination, and channeling her inner Buffy, it was only a matter a time before she started creating her own characters. Waiting for her chance at a job as a ninja assassin, Nana, meantime works out her drama, passion and sass with fictional characters every bit as sassy and kick butt as she thinks she is. **nana-maloneromance.net**